Tropic

MW00366888

By Zoe Chant
© Zoe Chant 2018
All Rights Reserved

All Rights Reserved

Shifting Sands Resort

This is book 5 of the Shifting Sands Resort series. All of my books are standalones (No cliffhangers! Always a happy ending!) and can be read independently, but many of these characters reappear in subsequent books, and there is a series arc. I suggest reading in order:

The Master Shark's Mate (A Fire & Rescue Shifters/Shifting Sands Resort crossover, occurs in the timeline between *Tropical Wounded Wolf* and *Tropical Bartender Bear*)

Firefighter Phoenix (A Fire & Rescue Shifters novel, has scenes set at Shifting Sands Resort, and occurs in the timeline between *Tropical Christmas Stag* and *Tropical Leopard's Longing*)

Chapter 1

THE LAST NOTES OF HER song were fading out of the room as Saina rose carefully from the foot of the bed.

The man at the other end of the bed remained still, one arm flung back on his pillow as he drooled on it. Saina nudged him with a finger and decided with relief he would probably sleep for a while. Her lullaby had done its work, and he'd fallen asleep without laying one greasy finger on her.

If she was lucky, he'd be snoring for a few hours, and wake up not the slightest bit wiser for his little nap, every memory of Saina and her music nothing more than a distant fantasy. She gathered the skimpy dressing gown around her shoulders and drew in a breath.

It was a big room, for a boat, but it wasn't big enough to hide much in. The safe in the closet gave her a moment of pause, but she knew that what she was really after wouldn't fit in the shoebox-sized compartment, so she continued her hunt until she found the suitcase under the bunk. It was locked, but too ridiculously heavy for its size to be clothing. The handcuff hanging open off the handle made Saina certain this was her goal.

She slipped her hairpin kit out of her dark, upswept hair and wriggled it into the lock, grateful that it wasn't a digital system. A few careful movements, listening diligently, and the tumblers fell away and clicked open. Saina unsnapped the clasps and tipped the lid back to expose bricks of pale gray, plastic-wrapped, just as it had been described.

This was it.

She sat back on her heels. She hated this whole job, every part of it was distasteful and wrong, even if the people on this yacht were all low-life smugglers who deserved no better. But her directions had been very specific and her Voice... her Voice *needed* her. No one else was going to come to her rescue, so it was up to Saina.

She went to the closet and got the lurid pink carry-on she had bought the week before, emptying its contents on the floor.

The bricks all but filled it, leaving room for one dress smashed on top, and her evening purse with her phone and makeup. The rest of the clothing, she stuffed into the handcuffed suitcase, shoving what was left to the very back of the closet.

Saina paused at the doorway and cracked the door, and was glad to see that the short hallway was empty. Sounds of carousing still came from the lounge towards the bow of the yacht, and she crept down the stairs towards the stern, pulling the luggage behind her as quietly as she could manage.

Two guards were standing outside the door out onto the back deck, smoking cigarettes and talking loudly.

Saina observed them through the windows, and looked past them to the dinghy tied along the side of the boat. It was pitch black out, in the very early hours of the morning. The tropical air was warm and thick with humidity. She suspected that a storm was coming.

Saina chewed on her cheek for a moment, considering her options. There weren't many. She sighed, sucked her breath in, loosened her dressing gown, and sauntered out of the door like she owned it.

Her appearance arrested their conversation, and she heaved a dramatic sigh, nearly upsetting her breasts out of the skimpy lingerie she was wearing. "Good evening, boys," she singsonged.

"It's that lounge singer Anders picked up at Jaco yesterday," one of them recognized.

"And what a bore that guy was," Saina said, giving them both appraising looks. Anders hadn't gotten anything more from her than a nap, but they wouldn't know that. She put one hand on her round hip and inspected her fingernails on the other.

They stared, cigarettes hanging from the edges of their mouths, before exchanging looks. Saina immediately dubbed them Skeptical and Hopeful in her head, based on their expressions.

Skeptical eyed her overloaded rolling luggage curiously, while Hopeful couldn't stop staring at the cleavage spilling out of the frilly little number she was wearing. Saina turned her attention on Skeptical, humming lightly under her breath.

"You looking to give us a little private show?" Hopeful suggested gleefully.

Saina answered with a few bars of an appropriate pop song:
"Are you looking
For a good time?
Have you got yourself
A thin dime?"

By the time she hit the second chorus, they were both swaying in place, the smile on Skeptical's face as broad and entranced as Hopeful's.

She kept singing as she went to work, persuading them with her song that nothing out of the ordinary was happening. There was nothing to see, they were simply lost in a simple fantasy of their own imagination. It would have been easier to simply drown them than to keep singing, like any one of her sisters would have, but Saina couldn't bring herself to do that.

Not even to drug-running scumbag mercenaries like this.

She pulled the pink bag behind her to the stern of the ship and lifted the cowling off the inboard motor. It took only a few strong yanks to disconnect the fuel and easy-to-reach electronics, and Saina used a fire extinguisher to dent the ignition mechanism so it wouldn't be an easy fix. The last thing she wanted was for them to be able to follow her. A glance showed that the disruptions to her song as she worked hadn't broken the spell over Skeptical and Hopeful, but she knew she didn't have much time or breath left.

Hauling the dinghy down from its rack and getting it over the side of the boat was a Herculean task, and Saina wished, not for the first time, that sensible shoes fit with the image she was trying to attain.

The dinghy splashed into the water, and Saina struggled to get the heavy luggage over after it, her song stuttering with the effort.

Then, as she drew in breath to get Skeptical and Hopeful back on track, her luck ran out.

On the deck above, there was a sudden shout and Saina looked up in alarm to spot another guard, this one with a girl hanging on his arm, dressed much as she was and looking vacant and tipsy.

Saina weighed her options. She wasn't sure that she could enspell the guard before others came to his alarm cry, and she wasn't sure how many more she would be able to sing insensible — she'd spent more of her energy than she anticipated. Instead of standing her ground, she kicked off her heels and vaulted over the edge of the boat into the wobbly dinghy. She flipped out the choke and yanked the tiny outboard to life.

The guard's shouts intensified, and Saina heard others answer. Hopeful and Skeptical shook off the last of her song in confusion. Frantically, she pointed the dinghy away from the yacht and kicked it up to high gear, cursing its powerless motor and slow speed.

Still, the yacht and the shouting began to drop away in the darkness behind her, and Saina breathed a sigh of relief. Maybe she would actually get away with this. Maybe...

Distant shots fired and bullets shattered the air around her. Saina dived to the bottom of the inflatable boat, covering her head and biting her lip against her cries of fear as they blasted around her for a length of time that seemed impossibly long. They couldn't see her in the darkness, so the shots were wild, and she knew that was her only saving grace. As it was, the boat lurched sickeningly and she knew it had been hit. She could only hope that it had multiple flotation pockets, and that what hadn't been compromised was enough to keep her afloat until she could get somewhere safe.

The motor hummed blissfully on, pushing her further and further away from the disabled yacht, and the shots became more sporadic as the shouts got more distant. Saina's cries of fear turned to sobs of pathetic relief as she thought she might escape with her life.

She crouched again, leaning to one side as the boat, clearly deflating on the other side, tipped and sagged. She scanned the water ahead, hopeful for lights, but saw nothing.

Behind her, another few shots rang out, and she was driven forward, nearly out of the boat, as pain and fire bloomed to one side of her back.

Chapter 2

BASTIAN DREW IN A DEEP breath of salty air. It was already windy, and he could smell the storm that was coming, though the sky above was still clear and sunny.

A sensible dragon would be taking cover, going to ground while the winds were too high to fly in. It was the sort of day to curl in one's hoard and count precious things, while the weather became wet and unfriendly.

But Bastian was no kind of sensible dragon.

In human form, he passed the empty pool, double-checking that the lounge chairs had all been secured and the towel cabinets were shut and latched. The bottles of sunscreen and lotion had all been stashed away, and the kickboards and pool floats were all behind closed doors. The sign declaring no lifeguard was on duty was already up, flapping noisily in the rising wind. Bastian grinned at it. A storm, rare here, meant a day off, and he was going to make the most of it.

He walked along the strangely bare deck. The few guests, like dragons, would be tucked away in their safe cottages, avoiding the wind and weather. As for the other staff, Bastian had no idea where they were, but he was just as glad not to encounter them and have to explain where he was going.

The steps down to the beach were littered with loose sand and Bastian shifted as he walked down them. One step was a sandaled foot, the next, a claw that spanned three of the white concrete steps. He may not be the largest dragon from his family, but he was far from the smallest. His scales gleamed green and gold, faceted like jewels.

Bastian paused at the lifeguard tower, taking a moment to appreciate the familiar view. The beach swept to either side, white sand stretching to meet sapphire water. The little beach bar was shuttered up, all the chairs safely inside. The dock was empty; the resort owner, Scarlet, had not yet replaced the boat that had been destroyed the week before.

He swiveled his head to look behind him. He was tall enough in dragon form to look easily onto the tiled pool deck, a useful trait as a lifeguard that enabled him to watch both swimming areas. Above the pool deck, the vacant bar deck looked down, and above that the restaurant deck. The steep structure of the Costa Rican island meant the resort was built in tiers, and it gleamed white in the sun.

The palm trees framing the pool were beginning to whip in the building wind, and Bastian could see the dark clouds beginning to gather behind the crest of the hill above him.

A dragon face wasn't arranged for grinning, but Bastian's inner human certainly was.

He had the day for himself.

He had the wide ocean for himself.

He walked down by the dock, where the ocean fell away more quickly than the swimming and sunbathing area and he could wade in and begin swimming almost at once.

At first, the swimming was awkward, clawed feet and powerful legs were not arranged for paddling, and wings, even tucked tightly against his side, dragged on the waves and wind.

Then Bastian sucked in a deep breath and dived, pulling all his limbs against his body and letting his massive tail propel him fully under.

No longer divided between air and ocean, he cut through the water as if he'd been born there, not a creature of fire, but of saltwater.

He had to surface near the breakwater; it grew too shallow there to stay beneath the waves, and he climbed over the rocks and paused, shaking water droplets off his big head and spreading his massive wings before he tucked them against his body again and returned to the element he preferred.

Fish scattered before him, and a pod of dolphins gave him wide berth, but Bastian paid them no mind. His human had eaten well from the resort kitchen and he had no need for legless prey this fine morning.

He was on a different kind of hunt, instead, and as he drifted along the sandy ocean floor, still holding his breath, he closed his eyes and let other senses take over.

At first, there was nothing, then, like distant musical notes, he felt the first tingle of treasure.

His lungs cried out for air, and Bastian oriented himself and returned to the surface to refill. However he loved the water, he still required air, like any dragon.

He dived down in the direction of the pull once he had sucked in a big breath.

The bit of treasure gave itself easily up to his big claws, digging down through the deep sand, and Bastian did a lightning fast shift so he could tuck it into his human form's belt pouch and shift back before he opened his senses to the next one.

Each time he returned to the surface for air, the waves and wind were rougher and rougher, once even breaking directly into his face as he was sucking in his breath.

He coughed and sputtered, thinking wryly that his family would feel vindicated if he died by drowning. That alone made him stubbornly decide to stay out in the storm. He floated at the surface, bobbing on the giant swells as he refilled his lungs and prepared to dive again.

A sudden wave of treasure sense broke over him more strongly than the wave of saltwater had. It dwarfed the little tingles that had called him earlier, and Bastian almost swamped himself responding to it.

There was a shark, he realized, as he dove back into the water; then he was surprised to sense another through the waves, until he realized that beneath the treasure sense was something else: blood.

He was not quite as fast as a shark, but Bastian put every ounce of his swimming strength into cutting the distance between his goal and himself.

By the time he got there, swimming up from beneath, there were three sharks circling what Bastian realized was a half-deflated dinghy, adrift without power and reeking of treasure and the iron tang of blood.

He could not roar underwater, nor flame the sharks, but he could growl, and the water took the vibrations of his claim to the interlopers.

The sharks circled one last time in confusion, then retreated some distance, continuing to swirl just out of his reach.

Bastian had no interest in them, and considered them no threat. Even without flame, he was a dragon, many times their size and strength, and no stranger to the ocean. He had claws like swords, and his jewel-faceted scales were solid protection against their teeth.

He surfaced to inspect his spoils, refilling his lungs.

The sad, wilted dinghy had clearly taken a beating, and it was being tossed on the wild waves, making it difficult to get close. Bastian's treasure sense was threatening to overwhelm him. There was something precious and rare here.

When a wave washed over the dinghy, sloshing into the bed of the boat and what lay there, instinct made Bastian open his mouth and challenge the ocean itself with a roar. This was his, his treasure, his to crown his hoard with.

The uncaring ocean answered by slapping another wave at him, driving the half-limp boat up against his chest.

Finally, Bastian could look into the boat itself, and he dismissed the lurid pink suitcase that was deforming the bottom of the boat without a second thought; his treasure was not in the heavy luggage. It was the figure, a limp woman wearing something flimsy and soaking wet, plastered to every lush curve. Her long dark hair was loose around her shoulders like a cloak. She was face-down in the boat, barely breathing, and even in the storm-dark, Bastian could see that blood had dyed the water in the boat dark crimson.

He carefully rolled her over, using a dragon claw like a surgical tool, and her face was the most beautiful golden color that he had ever seen.

This is our mate, he realized in wonder.

His human added anxiously, *She's been shot!*

Bastian could see that she had a wound, still oozing sharp-smelling blood, just above her heart. His human was alarmed at the amount of the blood she must have lost so far, but Bastian only knew that she was every treasure he had ever sought, and that he must take her safely to his hoard and give her everything that he had.

Another wave threatened to rip the sinking boat away from him, just as the clouds above opened up and began to drench them in rain.

Bastian snatched the woman up into his forearms as the tortured boat began to sink, and his human helpfully suggested how to keep her above the water without jostling her injury further.

We don't know if that bullet is still in her, his human warned him, but Bastian didn't need a reminder to treat her gently.

He couldn't fly with her, not through weather like this, so he continued on his back, using his tail to propel them. Here, along the surface, their progress was agonizing slow, and waves broke over them several times, washing away the blood as they traveled. Bastian felt like he could hear a song at intervals, low beneath the roar of the storm.

It was hours of this unpleasant travel, feeling the weak beat of her heart against the scales of his chest, before Shifting Sands came into view once more. Bastian lifted her into one forearm as his back legs found purchase under him. The wavebreak was as tall as he was, but he wrapped his wings forward around her protectively and carried her carefully to shore.

The wind was finally beginning to die down as he got her up to the shelter of the bar. Tex was there, taking stock of the storm damage. If he was surprised to see Bastian away from the beach in dragon form, that was nothing to the surprise on his face when Bastian slowly lowered his prize onto the floor, bleeding and wet.

Chapter 3

SAINA DRIFTED THROUGH dreams of waves and wilderness. At one point, she thought she was being carried by a jeweled giant, but all the fairy tales faded into a hellish landscape of pain and misery with every jostle and wave. She tried to sing, desperate to convince the giant she was a friend, to spare her, but a storm ripped the words from her lips.

She woke later, hard tile beneath her. A shirt folded beneath her head smelled comfortingly of saltwater and sweat.

There was pressure at her shoulder, but the pain was pleasantly distant for the moment.

"She's stopped bleeding!" It was a voice that was both unfamiliar and familiar, all at the same time.

Someone was binding her up, she realized. She kept her eyes shut and her breathing shallow. The voice didn't sound threatening, but she knew better than to think that meant anything. She wasn't safe here. Assuming she was would only lead to disappointment.

There were others nearby, too; she could hear their murmurs in a confused jumble: "Who would have shot her? Who is she? Could it be the cartel?"

"Bullet went through her," a rough voice with no welcome said. "Gotta be thankful for that."

"What is going on?" This new voice was a woman, sharp with authority and impatience.

"Bastian found a woman adrift in a sinking boat, all shot to heck." That voice was a Southern drawl.

"That is just what this day needed," the authoritative woman said, her voice closer. "What sort of boat?"

There was no attention being paid to Saina now, so she carefully drew in a breath and began to hum quietly. She was in danger here. Her only hope was to make them think she wasn't a threat. She wasn't sure if she was singing a seduction or a lullaby; she only knew that she was among strangers, that strangers were never benevolent, and she had to use the only defense she had to disarm them. Her shoulder was beginning to hurt in earnest now.

"It was an inflatable dinghy, out of gas and half-deflated." That was the voice she was thinking of as her savior. Bastian, apparently. "No markings, just a generic raft like you'd find on any yacht in the area. She was alone in it, with some luggage."

Her luggage! Saina breathed in a hopeful breath before resuming her faint, subtle song.

"Did you check the luggage for identification?"

"It sank," Bastian said apologetically, and Saina's heart sank with his statement. Her Voice would be gone from her forever.

Her song took a keen of grief that she didn't intend, and it drew attention she didn't want.

"Hey," Bastian said eagerly. "You're awake!"

Saina let her eyes flutter open. She couldn't tell how much of a spell she'd been able to cast; everything was distant and fuzzy with pain and confusion. Judging from the way he was gazing down at her, she'd been singing a seduction. She could expect the adoration to dissolve into confusion as her song faded, but there should be a short window of charity before it was gone completely.

What she didn't expect was her own reaction.

He was the most gorgeous man she had ever laid eyes on, with a jaw like a superhero, and arresting golden eyes. Sun-bleached hair was tousled over a tanned brow, and he had the most perfect nose she'd ever seen on a man. He was wearing a lifeguard uniform and she didn't have to feign a weak, grateful smile.

"My hero," she said musically, driving all her energy into the words.

The effort of it drained her to the bones, leaving her gasping as pain flooded over her.

"Shhh," Bastian said, gazing down at her like she'd unrolled the ocean. "Lie still, you're hurt..."

As he faded into blackness, Saina found herself regretting the unconsciousness because she wouldn't be able to gaze back into those beautiful eyes any longer.

Chapter 4

"It's a mercy she's asleep again," the strange man with tattoos and scars told Bastian. "Bullet wounds hurt. But she's a shifter, sure as shit, because she's healing like one."

"Who are you, exactly?" Bastian asked, still feeling stunned by the woman's brief green-eyed gaze.

He had very mixed feelings about the man already; on the one hand, he'd been remarkably knowledgeable about bullet wounds, which was an area that lifeguard medical training hadn't been thorough on.

On the other hand, Bastian was the only one who should be touching his mate and he irrationally wanted to punch the stranger.

"Wrench," the man said briefly and unhelpfully.

"He kidnapped Jenny," Travis, the resort handyman, added merrily.

Bastian gave the handyman a quizzical look. The lynx shifter handyman certainly wasn't treating the stranger the way Bastian would have expected him to treat a man who had kidnapped his mate.

"To be fair," Jenny added, as the mate in question, "he let me go."

Scarlet made a displeased noise that was part sigh and part growl. "Let's get her inside somewhere, and get to work cleaning up the resort. The Civil Guard will be here shortly for our other uninvited guest; we can have them take her back to the mainland with them."

"No!" Bastian said furiously, drawing his hands into fists.

The staff stared at him.

"Finders, keepers?" Tex, the Southern bear shifter bartender, teased. His own mate, Jenny's identical twin sister Laura, was standing next to him and she chuckled.

Bastian kept himself from growling at the innocent remark. "She's my mate. She stays on the island."

While the rest of the gathered staff gave exclamations of disbelief, congratulations, and surprise, Scarlet threw up her hands in disgust.

"That is just what we need," she said in frustration. "This is a business, not a dating club, and I've already taken one charity case today." She glared pointedly at Travis, Tex, and Wrench, who all sobered at her gaze. To Bastian, she said, "Put her in cottage eighteen and try to keep her from bleeding all over the sheets. And I don't want you mooning over her all day, we've got a beach to clean up. We have jobs, people!"

Her footsteps away across the open bar floor were angry and fast, and her absence left the room feeling larger.

"I can keep an eye on her," Jenny offered kindly.

"I'm sure Lydia won't mind if we borrow one of her dresses," Laura added diplomatically. "They look about the same size."

Bastian realized that his mate was very scantily dressed, and that Wrench was trying very hard to keep from letting his gaze linger too long on the nearly-naked curves of her golden skin.

He managed not to bare his teeth at Wrench, appreciating his efforts, but when the other man offered to help carry her, Bastian simply gathered his mate into his arms and let Wrench and Jenny handle the doors and blankets.

As he settled her limp form into the bed, he smoothed her dark hair back over the pillow and lay a single kiss on her perfect forehead. Everything was right with the world, now that she was here.

Chapter 5

SAINA FELT BETTER THE second time she woke.

The pain in her shoulder was considerably less, and she didn't feel as weirdly adrift and weak as she had before.

She was also in a much more comfortable bed, with big fluffy pillows under her head. A tropical print quilt was pulled up to her shoulders, and she found that the distasteful lingerie had been replaced by a simple, comfortable sundress.

"You're awake!"

A lovely, curvy black woman was sitting at a desk next to the bed, holding a sheaf of papers open in a manila folder. She looked friendly enough, but Saina knew better.

Saina struggled upright, as the woman rose and tried to stop her. "You're hurt, stay still!"

But being upright gave Saina more breath, and she opened her mouth and sang a few notes of a love song lullaby.

"Easy nights,
Northern lights,
Open your heart,
The lines on your chart..."

The woman looked at her quizzically. "I'm Jenny," she said, completely unmoved. "You shouldn't be sitting up, but you do have a lovely voice."

Saina blinked at her. Her gift didn't tend to be as strong with women, but she hadn't met a person yet that a simple sleep song had so little impact on. Jenny didn't even yawn.

"I'm Saina," she said uncertainly, abandoning her plan to put Jenny to sleep and try to escape. Her shoulder hurt wickedly. "Thank you?"

"You should lay back," Jenny scolded her. "You don't want to open the wound again. Saina is such a beautiful name!"

"It's better," Saina lied, but she let Jenny fluff her pillows and tip her back onto them. "Saina is Hindi for princess," she added.

"We'll let Bastian be the judge of how much better you are," Jenny told her, unconvinced. "He'll be so happy to see you awake."

"Bastian," Saina tasted his name in her mouth. "He's the lifeguard with the golden eyes?"

Jenny's smile was sparkling and oddly smug. "Yes. He found your boat sinking in the middle of a storm, lucky for you." She had an easy Californian accent, and a kind smile.

Saina didn't trust it for a moment.

She looked around the room. She was in a small, beautifully appointed bedroom with big French doors opening out onto a little porch. "Where am I?" There were, at least, plenty of exits.

"This is Shifting Sands Resort," Jenny explained. "A shifters-only vacation resort off the coast of Costa Rica."

Saina's hands made fists in the tropical quilt. "Shifters?" she asked, as innocently as she could manage. It was unnerving not to have her music to simply make this woman automatically like and trust her. Maybe the pain of her injury was making it work incorrectly.

Jenny gave her an amused look. "You wouldn't be healing that quickly if you weren't one, too," she said. "You don't have to hide who you are here."

Saina gazed back in consternation, not admitting anything. "What kinds of shifters?" she asked suspiciously.

"All sorts," Jenny said with a laugh. "I'm an otter shifter." She said it with wonder, as if she weren't used to the idea yet. "My mate is a lynx shifter. My sister is a wolf, and her mate is a bear."

Saina wondered what Bastian was, with those bottomless golden eyes, but didn't want to ask. "Your... mate?" she asked, instead.

Jenny's face took a soft, distant look. "For shifters, there is one person, one perfect mate. They know each other at once, as if their souls recognize each other."

It sounded lovely. And romantically ridiculous. Saina wasn't even sure she believed in love, let alone love at first sight.

"You... don't know about mates?" Jenny added, coming fully back to the conversation.

Saina refrained from scoffing that it sounded like a fairy tale. "I'd heard of them," she admitted. She didn't have to add that she'd never thought they existed. It seemed more likely that Jenny was under some other kind of magical influence.

Jenny's eyes danced, like she had a delightful secret that she wanted very much to share. "I'll let Bastian tell you more," she said, gathering her papers. "I know he'll want to know that you're awake."

When she left, Saina slipped carefully out of the bed. The view from her porch was out over the resort, the roofs of other little buildings like the one she was in spread out below her. There was jungle to her right, ocean before her, and just visible through the trees to her left, a gleaming white fortress that must be the restaurant and bar. The sun was just beginning to set, turning the sky gold and rose.

Saina leaned against the deck railing and closed her eyes to listen to the quiet sounds of distant ocean.

"Saina?"

His voice gave her a crazy little thrill to her toes, and Saina knew before she turned that her lifeguard had returned.

He was standing in the doorway, looking nervous and excited. Saina was equal parts relieved that her magic wasn't entirely gone, and surprised. The effects of her song should have faded away by now, but he was clearly still utterly besotted with her. It made her feel unexpectedly guilty.

"Jenny said your name was Saina," he said, adoration in the way he said it. Then he scowled in concern. "And you should be in bed!"

"I'm fine," she said, with a practiced silky smile. "You don't have to worry for me."

His scowl melted. "Let me at least check it," he breathed.

Saina sat at the edge of the bed and let him peel the medical tape back and check under the swaths of bandage that covered her shoulder front and back. His gentle touch was surprisingly disturbing to her calm, sending tingles of sensation through her skin. Had she managed to enchant *herself* with her injury-addled song?

"Well?" she asked, looking up into his face.

The eye contact obviously unbalanced him. He gazed down at her and stammered, "It's, it's, looking, coming along nicely. Healing up well. It looks... good."

Saina made herself smile at him. Whatever the reason, she would have one unquestionable ally here, then. She had to remind herself firmly that this was in her nature, that she ought to be grateful for this unexpected enchantment, not feel guilty about it. Even though she didn't understand how she had managed to cast an enchantment like this at all. It was nothing like her usual siren magic.

Chapter 6

SAINA.

Even her name was beautiful, as lovely and unique as she was. Her voice had a faint British-Indian accent.

Standing against the sunset, she was a dark silhouette, with long, loose hair to the middle of her back. She was neither short nor particularly tall, with lush curves in all the right places. Lydia's dress was flattering on her, a swish of embroidered white fabric to her knees, and Bastian wanted nothing more than to peel her out of it, lay her down on his hoard and claim her outright.

He wrestled his dragon back, checking her bandages, and was happy to find that her wounds were healing more swiftly than he'd expected.

"You must be hungry," he said, once he'd taped it all carefully back on, every electric touch tantalizing and tempting.

"I'm famished," Saina said, as if it hadn't occurred to her before.

His dragon was pleased with the idea of feeding her, but Bastian doubted she would want the cow carcass that *he* suggested.

"There's a buffet," Bastian said swiftly. "The best food. All gourmet. Chef is world-class, you won't be disappointed."

His dragon suggested feeding Chef to her if she found his food in any way lacking.

I doubt she's a cannibal, Bastian said chidingly.

We would love her even if she was, his dragon assured him.

Saina rose, and accepted the elbow that Bastian offered her with her good hand.

"You're okay to walk?" he verified. "I could... carry you."

She laughed, and her laugh was like music. "I assure you that won't be necessary."

She had to walk carefully on the gravel path; it was getting dark, and once she stumbled and hissed in pain, her hand tightening on Bastian's elbow.

When they arrived at the restaurant, he put her at the best table. Scarlet didn't encourage the staff to sit in the restaurant, preferring that they take their food and eat it privately, but at that moment, Bastian would have faced down her wrath. This was his mate, and he had every intention of feeding her in style.

There were only a few guests at other tables, and the white bandages, stark against Saina's golden skin, drew just a few curious stares.

Bastian's baleful glare put those to a swift end.

"Stay here. I will fetch you whatever you like," he said, settling her in the chair and not liking how strained her face looked.

"Oh," she said. "Some fruit would be lovely. Maybe some fish? I'm not picky, and it all smells amazing."

Bastian was reluctant to leave her, and he piled her plate as swiftly as he could with a slab of baked fish, every kind of fruit the buffet had to offer, and a serving of fragrant saffron rice. He arranged it as pleasingly as he could, stealing a bit of garnish from the buffet display for the finishing touch. He was trying to work out whether he should put her dessert on a separate plate when his dragon growled in warning.

Dessert forgotten, Bastian returned to his mate's table at a trot, to find the head waiter, Breck, dancing attendance on his Saina.

The leopard shifter was gazing at her in clear adoration, and Saina — his Saina! — was smiling back encouragingly.

His intended presentation forgotten, Bastian dropped the plate before his mate hard enough to make the food jump and muscled his way between Breck and the table, bristling with challenge. One of the chairs in his way toppled over backwards.

"Your work here is done," he growled.

Breck reacted with unexpected defiance.

"I'm here to take the lady's drink order," he said, not backing down.

"The lady is here with me," Bastian snarled.

"Maybe she shouldn't be..." Breck retorted, fists balled at his side.

He was dimly aware of the other guests in the room, some of them standing in alarm, some of them growling. He was going to tear Breck limb from limb, destroy the interloper, protect his treasure...

And then Breck was chuckling and putting up hands of mock truce, and everything was surprisingly fine. The waiter wasn't a threat, there was no threat, there was only peace, like the comforting rhythm of the ocean. His mate was standing, he realized, and she was singing.

Guests returned to their meals as if nothing had happened. Breck cheerfully picked up the knocked over chair, and said, "I'll have your drink right out."

Bastian watched him go, baffled, then turned to catch Saina, now silent, as she swayed and nearly fell.

"I'm confused," he confessed to her, lowering her carefully back into her chair and pulling up his own chair.

She was breathing hard. "I shouldn't have done that," she said, despair in her sea green eyes. "It was just a habit..."

"What did you do?"

"It was an accident," Saina said wearily, and Bastian couldn't bring himself to press her to explain. Instead, he lifted a fork and speared a triangle of pineapple. He could still feed his beloved.

Chapter 7

SAINA HADN'T INTENDED to ensnare the waiter, it had just been a matter of a little musical note to strengthen her request.

It was the kind of thing her sisters did without thought, and though she didn't tend to do the same herself, she had been so baffled by her lack of influence on the otter shifter that she'd been curious to give her gift a test on someone else.

She had been gratified to see that her power was still intact, but the waiter had reacted more strongly than she'd expected. Bastian's reaction was even more over the top, a crazy-protective rush to defend her that Saina hadn't expected at all; her song hadn't been focused on him whatsoever. Saina couldn't decide if her magic was unpredictable in this place, or if she simply wasn't controlling it as well as she ought to because of her injury.

She could stop the chaos, of course, but it meant getting to her feet and singing a counterpart to the strife, a sweet, lilting lullaby that soothed everyone in earshot.

The conflict dissolved away to not even memory, and the waiter left to fetch her drink while Bastian sat and tried to feed her from her plate.

After just a few bites, she took the fork from him and insisted on feeding herself. Bastian watched her intently.

"Your chef is as good as you claimed," she said, several bites into the flaky fish. Some of her exhaustion faded with the food.

Bastian looked as pleased with her praise as if he'd cooked it himself. "We're lucky to have him."

Saina could see the questions in his eyes, behind the infatuated obsession she still convinced she had put there, and she moved to intercept them.

"This whole place is simply lovely," she said honestly. "Tell me more about it! Jenny said we were in Costa Rica."

Bastian nodded. "The whole island is privately owned. Scarlet is the owner of the resort, she just leases the property. Most of it is wild jungle, but there's a private compound at the other end, and an airstrip on the north side. We get charters in a few days a week."

"You're the lifeguard?" It was a question with an obvious answer; Bastian was still wearing his uniform and had a first aid kit at his waist.

He nodded. "I watch the beach and pool."

"You'll have to give me a tour tomorrow," Saina said.

"I'd love to," Bastian said, a smile on his handsome lips.

She didn't want to stay longer than she had to, but it would be a day or two before her shoulder was completely healed. And the idea of a tour was strangely appealing, especially with Bastian as her guide.

She considered again the idea that she'd fallen under her own spell. Having him feed her had been unexpectedly erotic, and she found herself watching the way his hands moved, and the muscles in his jaw as he spoke. His hair begged for a hand to smooth it back, and Saina had to keep herself from doing it herself several times.

This was not how her magic was supposed to work. It was baffling enough that Bastian was still enchanted. *She* should be coolly indifferent, like a proper siren.

"I understand this resort is for shifters only?"

Bastian nodded, that unruly curl at his forehead bobbing with his earnestness. "There's been some talk about allowing humans to accompany shifter guests, but yes."

Saina glanced at the other scattered guests, all dining peacefully at other tables. She wondered what their forms were, what their ulterior motives were, and how they had gotten the kind of money it would take to vacation at a place this nice.

"It's good luck you found me," Saina said cautiously. "I'm very grateful."

Bastian's eyes glowed. "I don't think it was luck," he said, voice low and full of emotion. "I think it was destiny."

He would, Saina thought achingly.

She attempted to deflect the intensity. "Any other resort would have been quite baffled by how quickly I healed," she said with a light smile.

"Will you tell me what happened?"

He asked so respectfully that Saina found it difficult not to answer. She was actually surprised that no one had been more pointed about quizzing her over it. Did people show up at this resort half-drowned and with bullet wounds often?

She took a bite of a luscious scarlet strawberry to buy her a few moments. "It was a disagreement over ownership," she said evasively.

Bastian's eyes grew flinty. "Of you," he guessed.

Close enough, Saina thought. She looked at her nearly empty plate, flooded with guilt and shame, and couldn't answer.

How could she explain to this earnest man that it was supposed to be in her nature to sow strife and chaos in her wake? And why did it feel so wrong?

Bastian's hand covered her own, and she tried not to flinch at the electricity that coursed through her at his touch.

It felt like home, having his skin against hers, and she wanted to crawl into his lap and cry out all her troubles. He wanted to protect her; would it be so awful to let him?

She bit the inside of her cheek. This whole feeling of connection was false. When her magic finally faded, she wouldn't be more than a puzzling gap of memory to him.

"If I could help..." Bastian breathed.

Saina drew herself up. There was no way he was as good and as selfless as he seemed. "You can't," she said with a practiced smile. "But you could get me a plate of dessert!"

Bastian was out of his chair and back to the buffet before she could even add a little pout at the end.

She had cleared the rest of her plate by the time he returned bearing a dazzling array of sweets on three different plates. "I couldn't possibly eat all that!" She laughed at him.

He seemed to find that reaction pleasing, and when she insisted he enjoy one of the plates himself, agreed willingly. Even the way he ate was sexy, and when he licked sugar off his lips, Saina had to pinch herself to stay focused.

Each dessert was more decadent than the last, and when she put her fork down at last, she had to groan. "I should have skipped the last cream puff, but it was sooo good."

Bastian preened. "I shall let Chef know that you liked it."

"Please do," Saina said sincerely.

She washed the last rich bite down with a sip of the juice she hadn't even noticed the waiter bringing her earlier.

With the sip, and the reminder of her true nature, the exhaustion that had been barely at arm's length came rushing back. Saina's shoulder ached again.

It didn't go unnoticed.

"You should rest," Bastian told her. "Let me take you back..." his hesitation was obvious. Saina waited for him to insist they go back to his own room, but he finished: "...to your cottage."

Could he really be that much of a gentleman? Saina had expected to have to sing him to sleep to keep her hard-won chastity. She was almost tearfully grateful for that grace, even while she was slightly disappointed.

"I'd like that," she said, not having to feign her weakness.

Every step back to her cottage jarred her shoulder painfully, and Saina was glad to have Bastian on her good side to lean against. When he picked her up to lay her into her bed, she let herself put her head against his broad shoulder for just a moment too long, and letting go again was more difficult than she imagined it could be.

He changed her bandage with swift, gentle fingers. "It's healing well," he said, sounding relieved.

"I'm mostly... tired," Saina said truthfully.

"That's to be expected. Sleep as long as you need," Bastian told her, tucking the light blanket carefully around her. "I'll know when you wake up."

Saina was too tired to ask how he would know, and let her eyes drift closed as she felt his lips chastely kiss her forehead.

This resort was like a guilty dream; people who didn't pry into her past or act like she was beholden to them, despite the fact that she owed them her life. No one obviously trying to hurt or use her.

Saina fell asleep wondering when the other shoe would drop.

Chapter 8

BASTIAN RETURNED TO the staff house feeling like his feet had wings of their own.

His mate. His beautiful, graceful, glorious mate was here, and his life felt complete.

She had accepted his food, and suggested he give her a tour of his domain, sure signs of acceptance. She was healing swiftly, and Bastian expected nothing but a full recovery as his courtship started in earnest.

"The Menagerie? Or Animal House?" Breck greeted him as soon as he stepped into the door of the big house most of the male staff shared.

"*Non sequitur*, much?" Bastian responded, puzzled but amused. Their earlier altercation was still confusing, but forgiven.

"We're trying to name the house before Scarlet labels it something bland like Palm House or Cliff Columns," Travis explained. "I'm surprised you're back here for the night."

"I'm going to veto Menagerie," Jenny said from the far couch. "Too suggestive."

"But Animal House is way too National Lampoon," Travis added.

"The Furever House?" Breck suggested.

Jenny made a gagging noise and Graham, the lion shifter gardener, grunted negatively.

"It sounds like a pet rescue," Travis scoffed.

Breck blew him a raspberry. "You come up with something," he said. "Who wants a beer?"

Bastian settled into his usual chair with a bottle of beer, enjoying the camaraderie of the staff and the warm glow that still lingered from being in the presence of his mate.

"The Zoo?" suggested Jenny.

The others considered until Travis reluctantly said, "Too many memories of Beehag's zoo," and they all murmured in agreement.

Alistair Beehag, the previous owner of the island, had captured shifters, forced them into their animal forms, and kept them in a cruel zoo. The resort staff had helped free them, almost a year ago, but memories of the angry, sometimes damaged, victims were still fresh. A gazelle shifter named Gizelle for lack of a previous name had been imprisoned since she was a child, and had no memories besides iron bars and torture. The odd, ageless woman was still skittish and sometimes outright incoherent.

"The Predators?" Bastian suggested.

"Jenny lives here now, and an otter isn't really a predator," Breck said thoughtfully.

Jenny bared her white teeth at him. "Says someone who isn't a fish."

"Sounds like a team mascot, not a house," Travis said dismissively. "Anyway, with luck, we'll be moving to our own place soon enough. I'm going to ask Scarlet if we can renovate one of the houses up the hill."

Jenny cuddled into his side and purred, "What a beautiful idea!"

"Don't ask Scarlet this week," Breck warned them. "She's in a terrible mood. She was already on edge after the World Mr. Shifter event, and the storm did nothing to improve matters."

"Tooth Towers," Graham suggested unexpectedly.

"Hmm," Breck said.

"I like it," Travis said.

"Meh," said Jenny, less enthused.

"If we don't decide on something, it'll end up being Grouch Gables or something," Breck reminded them.

"Why *aren't* you with your mate tonight?" Jenny asked Bastian frankly. "She hasn't rejected you, has she?" Beside her, Travis took her hand and squeezed it.

Bastian didn't take offense to the idea, shaking his head. "Our courtship is just beginning," he said patiently.

"Guh," said Breck. "Dragons." Then he leaned forward curiously. "Have you found out what she is?"

Bastian shook his head. "It's not important," he said dismissively.

"Your family won't be happy if she's not a dragon," Graham said sagely.

A spark of anger lit in Bastian at the reminder of his family. "It's not their business," he said sharply. "And what do you know about dragons or my family anyway?"

Graham, unfazed, only shrugged in reply.

"Stick to plants," Bastian growled at him.

He didn't stay long in the common room after that, but slunk away to his room, stewing over the unwelcome memory of his family.

Chapter 9

DAY DAWNED EARLY IN the tropics, and Saina woke to sunlight sending fingers of light through the curtains over the big French doors to the porch.

When she gave her shoulder an experimental roll, it barely hurt at all, and she was relieved to find that she felt refreshed after the good night's sleep.

She remembered Bastian's last words about knowing when she would wake, so she was not surprised when there was a knock on the door.

She was, however, surprised to find that it wasn't Bastian, but a tall woman with shockingly red hair pulled back in an unruly bun. She buzzed with power to Saina's senses, the air around her crackling faintly.

"You are Saina," the stranger greeted her without preamble or particular warmth. "I am Scarlet, the owner here." They exchanged a perfunctory handshake with Saina's good hand, and Scarlet gave Saina a swath of fabric that proved to be a new dress and a pair of underthings still in packaging.

"I understand you'll be staying with us for a while," Scarlet said, not hiding her displeasure and giving Saina an appraising look. "Are you interested in working?"

Saina swallowed her protest that she wouldn't be staying, standing up straight under the woman's scrutiny. "I can, ah, sing. Perform, I mean."

The woman's gaze grew flinty. "This isn't a *Vegas* resort," she said dismissively.

Stung, Saina wondered if the woman assumed she was a Vegas-style escort. It would be a valid guess, based on the clothing she had arrived in, she realized with chagrin. "Of course not," she agreed firmly. "But I can earn my keep."

"Can you wash dishes?" Scarlet asked skeptically, looking at Saina's hands doubtfully. "Make beds?"

"I'm not above hard work," Saina replied defensively. "I can do any of that, or help trim hedges or pull weeds."

"We have a landscaper," Scarlet said flatly. "We'll try you in the kitchen. On a *trial* basis." She looked at Saina's bandage and her voice softened. "When you are feeling up to it, of course. I don't mean to rush your recovery."

Briefly, Saina thought that the concern was genuine behind her cool face and polite words, and the idea unsettled her.

"I will also expect incidents like last night to remain at a minimum," Scarlet added then.

Saina felt her eyes widen and she swallowed. "You heard about that?"

Scarlet smiled without humor. "I know everything that happens on this island," she said dryly.

"I will make sure that doesn't happen again," Saina said with a shy, tentative smile. Not all siren charms relied on magic, she reminded herself. She didn't like how unpredictably her magic worked here, and she didn't like how dirty it made her feel to use her magic on people who had offered her nothing but charity.

Scarlet made a noise that may have been polite or simply skeptical, and turned to leave just as Bastian came running up the gravel path.

Saina didn't like to admit how her belly fluttered at the sight of him, or how weak her knees suddenly felt. He was so gorgeous and athletic looking, with shoulders like a wall, and strong swimmer's legs, shown off to advantage by his lifeguard uniform.

Scarlet looked from one to the other and said dryly to Bastian, "I believe you'll be wanting the rest of the morning off?"

Bastian grinned and managed to look sheepish at the same time. "Yes, ma'am," he said hopefully.

"Fine," Scarlet said without smiling. "But we're getting a new batch of guests with the charter plane this afternoon and I expect our lifeguard to be on duty when they are ready to enjoy the swimming."

She didn't wait for Bastian's affirmation, but turned her attention to Saina. "If you are feeling up to it, we could use your help cleaning up after lunch rush in the kitchen."

She didn't wait for Saina's answer either, but turned on her heel and stalked away.

Her exit took a tension that Saina hadn't even recognized with her, like the pressure before a storm, and it left a new one in its place as she was alone with the man who had saved her.

He smiled at her foolishly for an awkward length of time, and Saina found herself doing the same, until she recognized it. "You mentioned a tour," she suggested.

"Yes, of course. I'd love to show you around!" Bastian offered his elbow chivalrously.

Saina nearly took it, then realized that she was still wearing the dress she had worn the previous day and then slept in. "Oh, could you wait while I take a quick shower? I promise it won't take long."

"Of course," he said with effort.

She was gazing up at his face, so she could see his impulse to offer to join her, and watch him wrestle with his desire to remain appropriate. No other man under any siren song had ever demonstrated that kind of restraint. By this point, she expected him to be demanding his way into her bed, and she'd have to sing him to sleep to make her escape. Once again, she wondered why her powers were behaving so strangely; he certainly shouldn't still be enchanted, let alone acting like this.

She was faintly disappointed that Bastian hadn't made that kind of demand, and had to wonder if she wouldn't straight out welcome him there. It was an eye-opening revelation, as she retreated into the bathroom to wash.

She hadn't anticipated how exciting the shower would be, knowing that Bastian was just outside the door. Covered with bubbles, she couldn't keep her hands from drifting over her breasts a few extra times, and rinsing more intimate parts threatened to become a serious distraction as she wondered what he would look like out of his uniform. Then she imagined soaping those gorgeous shoulders, and her breath grew shallow and fast and she had to lean against the cool tile wall of the shower and get control of herself again.

Down girl, she told herself firmly.

She toweled off briskly, careful not to linger anywhere, then realized that she'd left her new clothing out in the bedroom.

Part of her wanted to saunter out naked and test Bastian's unexpected self-control, but most of her knew that would break her own tenuous restraint, so she cracked the door. "Ah, Bastian, could you bring me the clothes on the bed?"

"Of course!" He had been staring out the double doors over the porch and came swiftly with her request, slipping it through the door to her.

Any of her sisters would have given him a tantalizing tease, opening the door more than strictly necessary, but Saina only took the clothing and dressed efficiently out of sight. She didn't want to do more to the people here than she already had.

It's not real, she reminded herself firmly. *None of this is real, and you'll be gone in a day or two, so don't do anything stupid.*

Like fall in love...

Chapter 10

DRESSED IN A PATTERNED golden sundress, freshly showered, with her hair loose and wet over her shoulders, Saina was the most glorious treasure Bastian had ever seen. The early morning light made her glow, and her green eyes were more radiant than any sea glass he'd ever seen. She left the bandages off, and Bastian made himself look at her shoulder professionally.

"I think we can leave the bandage off this morning," he said, trying not to sound as flustered as he felt. The wounds were barely puckered scabs, and the skin around them already looked healthy, with no signs of infection.

She rolled her shoulder experimentally, wincing only once in the rotation. "It's better," she agreed.

Then she tipped her chin up to smile at him. "I believe you'll be my tour guide for the morning."

Bastian shared the resort with her as if it was all his own realm, an attitude he was sure that Scarlet wouldn't appreciate, but one she was not present to correct. They started at the top, where Scarlet's office presided at the top of the steep slope. From there, he pointed out the cottage roofs. "Tex and Laura are staying in that one, for now. The big one with the two porches, that's Magnolia's. She's one of our semi-permanent residents, you'll love her."

Saina made a small skeptical noise that made Bastian suspect she didn't have many female friends.

He led her down past the spa. Wrench and Travis were there, repairing some storm damage to the spa building finish, and Bastian was happy to show her off and introduce her.

"It's lovely to meet you," she said, and gravely shook their gloved hands.

He took a quick walk through of the garden, and braved Graham's wrath by picking one of the red bell-like flowers for Saina's hair.

"There's a greenhouse, there." He pointed to the diamond-sparkle roof through the trees. "We grow a good portion of our own food. And the tall white house is where most of the male staff lives. The ladies' staff house is the green one beyond."

They walked past the utilitarian hotel building for budget guests, and Bastian pointed out his old room in the windows.

They walked down to the entrance of the restaurant, and snagged egg bagels dusted with green onions and flakes of salmon from the buffet before making their way down to the bar level. The bar was open air, as most of the resort was, tucked under the restaurant deck. The bar tables and chairs overlooked the jewel of the pool. Twin waterfalls toppled from this level, framing a grand staircase with columns down into the sapphire water.

Walking past the bar led to the event hall, where Lydia held her sunrise yoga and they hosted semi-weekly dance events. "You'll meet Lydia next week," Bastian told her. "She's back home visiting family in Mexico and doing some sort of massage training."

The pool deck had a few guests sunning themselves, and Bastian was pleased with Saina's reaction to the pool itself. "It's the biggest pool I've ever seen," she said in awe.

"We hosted the World Mr. Shifter event just a week ago. The photographers said it was one of the most beautiful places they'd ever hosted a shoot." Bastian was as proud of the resort as if it had been his own ancestral home.

"I can see that," Saina agreed, appropriately impressed.

Then he could guide her down the steps to the beach itself, and if she had loved the pool, she was clearly moved by the picture-perfect white sand crescent.

"This must be where you work," she said, standing by the lifeguard tower. At some point over the sand, she had taken his hand, and they had fingers twined together.

"Well," Bastian said modestly, "I hardly ever use the tower. I'm usually in dragon form so I can see further, and keep an eye on the pool deck at the same time."

Her fingers in his turned to rock. "In what form?" she asked, frozen.

"Dragon," Bastian repeated, and he was surprised when she withdrew her hand and backed away from him, eyes wide and skin pale beneath her natural golden tone. "What is it?" He asked gently, suddenly afraid he'd done something wrong.

"You're a dragon," she said flatly.

"You didn't know about dragons?" Some cultures kept their dragons secret. Perhaps India was one of those. "I assure you, we are not simply mythological."

"I *know* about dragons," she spat, and Bastian felt as if his world was tipping unexpectedly.

Chapter 11

A DRAGON, SAINA THOUGHT. She hadn't expected Bastian to be a dragon. This changed everything.

She had finally felt like maybe she could take this place at face value, had even felt badly for her first instinct to try to control the people here who had been nothing but kind and generous.

She turned away, more disturbed by this revelation than she ought to be. She shouldn't care. She shouldn't care in the slightest for this man, let alone should she care what his shifted form was.

But despite her care, he'd gotten under her skin, she'd trusted his boyish smile and softened to his chivalrous actions. Dragon honor could be a tricky thing, she should know.

"Saina?" Even his voice sounded innocent.

"What family are you from?" she asked, chin high as she looked out over the turquoise ocean that lapped along the beautiful beach.

He hesitated so long that she made the mistake of looking back at him.

His face was so terribly dear to her already, and the pain on it now made her want to comfort him.

"I am from the Santa Rosa dragon family," he said, and he said it with so much guilt that Saina knew he had to know. He *had* to know what his family had done to hers.

"You *knew*," she said. "You knew all along. Did Keylor send you after me? I'm such an idiot. I can't believe..."

"Keylor?" Bastian said in surprise. "You know Keylor?"

Saina paused in her rant. His disbelief felt genuine, however much that didn't make sense.

"Who are you to Keylor?" she asked, taking one angry step towards him. She put music into her words, and added:

"Tell the truth,

Say it fair,

Speak it clear,

Don't lie, don't dare..."

It was one of her strongest songs, and backed by her betrayal and anger, she could feel it bind Bastian like iron as she held the last note.

"He is — was — my brother," he gasped, as if he were being squeezed.

Saina let the last note go and he blinked at her in consternation. "I am not accepted as family any longer, and I am not allowed to claim kinship or mention their name."

Saina furrowed her brows at him. "Explain," she said firmly. She drew in a breath and held it, in case he needed a second verse.

Bastian sighed. "I am... mentally unfit for the family. I was cast out when my deviance was discovered. The only way I would be permitted to return would be to marry dragon royalty."

"Deviance?" Saina pressed.

Bastian gestured with a hand, out to the ocean. "Water. I am a fire dragon, a creature of air and flame and fortune. But my treasure sense is... flawed, and I have an aberrant love of water that my kin could not accept. Worst of all, though I come from a proud lineage of warriors, I wanted to save people, and learn healing. I am in every way a perversion of dragonkind; they could not allow me to pollute the purity of the family with my association."

Saina chewed on this. "And Keylor?"

"My younger brother," Bastian said. "A proper dragon of fire and temper. He took my place as heir when I was thrown out. I haven't seen any of them in three years."

Saina turned back to the ocean to digest these revelations.

"What was that?" Bastian asked quietly. "Saina? What *are* you?"

Saina turned back to him. She believed that he'd told the truth about his exile, and she knew that her song had been unnecessary. He would have been genuine without her magic, she realized, and it shamed her that she had used it.

"Haven't you guessed?" she mocked gently. "I'm a siren."

He looked at her blankly and Saina sighed. "A mermaid, Bastian. I'm a mermaid."

He continued to stare.

Did he have to be so handsome and innocent? Saina wanted to brush his unruly hair back from his high forehead and plant a kiss there. "Come on," she said. "I'll show you."

She took one unresisting hand and led him out into the water. She didn't bother undressing, but waded out with him until the swells were chest deep, then she fell into the saltwater and shifted.

Chapter 12

BASTIAN LET SAINA LEAD him into the lapping waves, bemused by the depth of his own confession. He'd had every intention of telling his mate about his family disgrace, but he had hoped she'd have a chance to know him a little better before he divulged the extent of his exile and the depths of his depravity.

He certainly hadn't planned to tell her like that.

But he'd been as compelled as if he'd had Wonder Woman's lasso of truth wrapped around him, and she seemed to think that it was perfectly normal to be able to sing her will into anyone around her.

A siren, he thought in wonder. He'd been feeling so smug about how unknown dragons were, and she was something rarer and more mythical.

She is our treasure, his dragon said proudly. *There is nothing rarer or more valuable.*

Then, between one step and the next, she dived into the lightly lapping waves, and Bastian reached after her in alarm.

She surfaced beside him again, her long dark hair spilling back from her face, then swam beside him and flipped glimmering fins at him.

She was astonishing.

51

Her violet tail was more than just a simple flexible appendage; it was finery in jewel-faceted scales, longer than her legs had been by half. Feathery fins shimmered around her like veils, and when she moved, there were green and rainbow hues glittering beneath the patterned shades of purple.

Bastian had to swallow. Her breasts, bare, were as glorious as he'd imagined from all her various states of dress, and he had to remind himself repeatedly not to stare.

You should stare, his dragon urged him. *She is ours, and she is beautiful, and we should admire her.* (He was, not surprisingly, more impressed with her stunningly scaled bottom half than her curvy top half.)

"Come swim with me," she invited. Her voice was musical, but there was no compulsion to it.

"Don't sirens drown their victims?" Bastian said, trying to keep his voice light and the raging need in his blood from boiling over. He was grateful he was waist deep in the water now, because his erection would have been difficult to hide.

She raised an eyebrow at him, and while he was watching her face, flipped her fins to shower him with water.

Spluttering, he dived after her, to find that she had slipped further away, laughing and splashing.

Underwater, she was even more gorgeous than above, her graceful fins in mesmerizing motion, and she led him out to the wavebreak, and slipped over it into the surf.

Bastian hesitated only a moment before following her, and once past the reef, he shifted, diving fast and powerful through the water as the ocean floor fell away beneath them. She swam faster than a human swimmer, but not as fast as a dragon.

He was gratified by her wide-eyed surprise when he caught up with her.

She reached out as he passed, and her fingers were tantalizing brushing along his scales. He circled back to her, and she put wondering hands on his scaled nose.

You are so beautiful, she said in his head suddenly.

I was just thinking that, he told her, surprised and delighted to discover this new intimacy. Dragons could speak in this fashion with each other, but he had not known that he would be able to speak with mermaids this way, too. Was it only because she was his mate?

Take me deeper! she suggested.

She swam to the back of his head and held onto his horns. Bastian gathered his dragon body and kicked off with wings and legs before folding them back against him and letting his thick tail power them forward.

She was the barest tickle of fins at his head, but she was laughter and delight in his mind as they cut through the water, going deeper and darker below.

The wordless depths had been a place of peace before, but with his mate beside him, they became a new paradise. Schools of fish scattered before them, and a startled octopus darted away in a cloud of frightened ink.

It was several minutes before Bastian realized that he had unexpectedly had no need to return to the surface to breathe.

It's my gift, Saina told him. *Sirens can let anything breath underwater that they touch.*

I thought your voice was your gift, Bastian said bemusedly.

A girl can have more than one gift. Saina's mindvoice was sarcastic and dry.

Bastian's response was wordless gratitude and all the love and adoration in his big dragon heart.

He felt her withdraw from him, silent and non-receptive. Finally, she said, *Let's go back to the resort.*

There was an undercurrent of pain to her voice, and Bastian wondered if the swim had been too hard on her shoulder.

He took them back through the clear water, and rose out of the waves with her still clinging to his neck. She had shifted back to human form by the time he stepped onto the sand, and he shifted smoothly so that she was riding on his shoulders when he'd left the last lapping wave behind.

"Let me down!" she said, light laughter in her voice.

He crouched, and turned to catch her as she slipped from his shoulders.

He put her down on her feet, but no power in the world could have made him let go of her then. She was human, and dressed again in the golden sundress. Her skin was warm velvet under his fingers.

When he bent to kiss her, she froze for a moment, lips just parted under his, then gave a sigh of surrender and put her arms around his neck and kissed him back.

Chapter 13

SAINA COULDN'T FIGURE out how something could be so wrong and so right at the same time.

Bastian's arms were the most wonderful place that she'd ever been. He smelled like salt and safety, and Saina wanted to stay here, kissing him, forever.

No, she realized after only a moment, she didn't want to stay here. She wanted to drag him somewhere private and peel him out of his wet uniform, and why shouldn't she?

He wanted her. There was no mistaking the urgency of the erection he was trying not to obviously press against her as he claimed her mouth.

And she wanted *him*. She wanted him more than she'd ever wanted anyone in her life, so badly that she ached with it. The pain in her shoulder was the merest tickle compared to the fire that was smoldering in her loins.

"My cottage," she said, between kisses.

She'd never felt someone smile *while* they were kissing her, but Saina immediately decided this was one of her favorite things ever.

He swept her suddenly into his arms, making her squeak in protest and cling to his neck. Then he proceeded to carry her the entire way to her cottage, never pausing with his kisses.

He only almost dropped her once, during a particularly long, breathless kiss when he was climbing stairs at the same time, and Saina laughed and begged him to put her down.

"You are my treasure," he told her, and then they were at the door of her cottage and he finally had to put her down for lack of a free hand to open it.

She let him in almost shyly, and shut the door behind him as he shucked off his shirt and dropped the first aid kit he was wearing on a table.

He was so gorgeous, she thought, feeling weak. Her mouth was swollen with his kisses, and her heart was pounding.

His chest was like a sculpture, perfect tanned skin over muscles like mountains. Saina wanted to put her hands on it, but was suddenly, unexpectedly nervous.

"My treasure," Bastian repeated, looking adoringly at her.

Saina wanted to be that treasure he saw, she realized. She wanted it so badly.

And it was utterly wrong.

She didn't know how or why her enchantment had taken such a hold on him, but it had to be her magic that made him look at her that way. If she slept with him now, she was no better than any of her siren sisters... and he made her want to be better than that.

She stared at him, wrestling with the fire in her belly that urged her to do what they both wanted so badly, and the little voice that told her she would regret it forever.

He was waiting, invitation and tension in every plane of his amazing body, and she was just staring at him in growing consternation.

"Saina?" he said gently, when she didn't come to him.

"I can't do this," she said miserably.

He swallowed hard.

Saina opened her mouth. This was where she would sing him to sleep and make her escape. She could swim again; her shoulder barely ached at all.

Then she closed her mouth again.

That was the easy way. The siren way.

But it wasn't the *right* way.

Chapter 14

BASTIAN WATCHED SAINA struggle, fascinated and heartbroken by the array of emotions that crossed her beautiful face: guilt, pain, resignation, frustration, fear. He wanted to close the distance between them and gather her into his arms, to assure her that whatever crisis she was facing, he was hers. But something told him that would only make things worse, so he waited, leashing his desire and protective instinct to the best of his ability.

"I'm sorry," she said achingly. "I'm sorry you found me. I'm sorry I am who I am. I'm sorry I let you think this was something more than it was for so long. I'm just... so sorry."

Bastian blinked. "I'm not sorry I found you," he said at once.

"Don't," Saina breathed miserably. "Don't be so perfect."

Perfect? She thought he was perfect?

"Saina..." Something occurred to Bastian. "Have you ever been with... er, am I your *first*?"

Her face was a kaleidoscope of emotion.

It wasn't an obvious guess. She was lushly curved and exuded sexuality like a cat in heat to Bastian's senses. She had perfect flirtations that she could turn on in an instant, and she clearly knew exactly how to walk and smile for just the attention that she didn't seem to want. The clothing she had arrived in suggested the exact opposite.

But Bastian believed her when she sighed and admitted, "Yes. You would be."

She dropped into the chair and Bastian settled on the bed opposite from her.

"This would be much easier if I were like other sirens," she said in frustration.

"What are other sirens like?" Bastian asked, already disliking them for not being like her.

"Oh, you know," she said mockingly. "Seducing sailors, drowning people."

Bastian was fairly sure she wasn't really joking; there was too much bitterness in her voice.

"Tell me," he told her without judgment, wishing he could touch her.

She looked back at him unflinchingly, then lowered dark lashes over her sea green eyes. "I wish I were kidding," she said in a flat voice. "But every mermaid I've ever known but one was out only for themselves. We... don't have families like you do. Siren women form a loose pod, but our loyalty to each other is usually not strong."

"And the men?" Bastian had to ask.

"There are no male sirens," Saina said stiffly. She swiftly added, "Children of trysts are raised in the pod if they are girls, and abandoned on land if they are boys."

"Can all sirens sing like you?" Bastian asked, putting an unconscious hand to his throat as he remembered the compulsion of her song on the beach and the way she had defused the unexpected tension in the restaurant the night before.

She stiffened. "No, not all of us," she said, and her voice was full of grief and regret. "Most of us can sing a simple seduction, but not all of us have more complicated talents."

Bastian didn't press her and Saina gathered herself and went on.

"My grandmother was a singer like me. She used to tell me that the magic we could do came from our hearts, that sirens were meant for greater things. And when she was lost... I realized that she was the only reason our pod had stayed together as long as it had. Without Our Voice, we were lost. My sisters all left, free to pursue their own baser desires."

"Your Voice?" There was a significance to the title that Bastian couldn't define.

"It is the title for our matron, our leader if you like. I went after her, made a deal for her freedom, but it went badly."

Bastian had wondered how she ended up with a bullet hole, adrift in the middle of the ocean, and this started to explain it. He made a sudden connection. "Keylor. That's how you know Keylor."

"He swore he would free Our Voice if I did a job for him. A simple job, for someone with my gifts. And I got what he was after, too. But it sank with the dinghy. I'll never get it now, and I don't know another way to satisfy his demands."

Bastian could feel the fire of rage rising inside his chest. "He blackmailed you. He kidnapped your grandmother and blackmailed you for her release."

"He took her as a matter of debt," Saina elucidated. "I don't know the details, but he considered himself wronged and took her to satisfy his honor."

"He wouldn't harm her," Bastian assured her, knowing it was a pitiful assurance.

"Of course not," Saina agreed. "I know a little about dragon honor." She said it with disgust. "It's no wonder you all make such amazing lawyers."

"I would make a terrible lawyer," Bastian confessed.

Saina smiled at him, a crooked, genuine smile. "That's why I like you so much."

Bastian felt like his chest expanded seven times when she said it. "I want to show you something," he said impulsively, standing up.

Chapter 15

SAINA KNEW WHERE THEY would go before Bastian led
her to the staff house. A paper taped to the front door read
"Bachelor Barn." This was crossed out and beneath it, in different handwriting: "Crew Quarters." This was crossed out with a
side-note: "No Star Trek references!"

The common room was empty, sunlight streaming in
through the open curtains. The decor was decidedly dated and
80s style, but everything was clean and tidy, and the couch
looked comfortable.

Bastian's room was at the end of a short hallway on the top
floor; Saina guessed that this had originally been the master
bedroom from the floor plan. Rather than a standard bedroom
lock, it had a sturdy hasp with a keyed padlock on it.

Bastian unlocked it, then hesitated, one hand on the door-
knob. "I don't want this to be a surprise," he said awkwardly.
"I'm not sure how to explain it."

"I've known a few dragons," Saina said. "I know about their
hoards."

Bastian looked more uncomfortable, if possible. "It's not a
normal hoard," he said, and he looked so anxious that Saina
wanted to give him a hug. She squelched the uncharacteristic
impulse.

He probably had a puny hoard, by dragon standards. Saina braced herself for a few sparse jewelry boxes and a couple of brass goblets. Maybe the walls would be tapestries that weren't embroidered in gold.

She started to hum out of habit, wanting to ease Bastian's tension, and made herself bite her cheek to stop. She was done singing her way out of awkward places of her own making.

Bastian took a deep breath, and opened the door.

Saina sucked her own breath in, and stepped into his dazzling nest.

There were no tapestries on the walls at all, only fine fishing net bleached white, covering every wall and each inch of the ceiling. It was even over the windows, and sunlight glowed through the treasure that hung on it, turning the room into a rainbow.

There were a few golden necklaces and rings laid out on the dressers — the sorts of things that Saina had seen in other dragon hoards. But most of it was treasure from the ocean: sea glass, shells, shards of mother-of-pearl, pieces of brilliant coral. A tall brass vase stood in one corner, pitted and crusted with barnacles. An entire anchor filled another corner, more treasure displayed on it. There were sea stars and sand dollars, and old gold and copper coins, polished clean.

It had all been selected for beauty, not value, and the effect was utterly magical. Each piece had been placed as carefully as it had been collected; the room was completely in harmony with itself. It made a song rise up in Saina's throat that she had to stuff back with determination. She felt as if she had just come home.

Saina walked into the room in a daze. The floor was a fluffy, thick white carpet; her toes felt worshipped just wriggling in it. She couldn't help but wonder how awful it would be to vacuum sand out of it, and she hoped her feet were clean.

The bed was a monster of comfort, with about a hundred throw pillows in sea themes, and a glittery comforter that Saina recognized from a Bedding and Bathing catalog. It had been advertised for little girls' rooms; she hadn't even realized it was offered in a King size.

Bastian was watching her anxiously.

"Do you... like it?" he asked, as if he were being forced to and was dreading her answer.

Saina laughed, and couldn't keep her magic entirely out of the sound. "I love it," she admitted, trying to rein in the effect.

It was no good, Bastian was looking at her with that dazzled look she knew too well, worshipful and adoring.

He cleared his throat. "It's our tradition to gift our mate with the most valuable treasure from our hoard," he said formally.

Saina stared. His mate? She'd only tried to make him feel well-disposed to her, to be her ally in a strange place. Instead, he'd fallen harder for her than anyone she'd ever enspelled.

Bastian was holding a necklace made of massive gold links and rubies that didn't match with the rest of the hoard at all. "This was my coming of age gift," he said. "It is worth more than anything else here."

"Oh, oh, no," Saina said.

He blinked, looking at the necklace. "I know it's not very... elegant, but these are very rare rubies and it's all solid gold."

"No, no, no," Saina repeated, trying to retreat to the door and nearly tangling herself in the fishing net beside it instead. Sea glass chimed reproachfully at her.

Bastian looked crushed, and stared at the necklace in distaste. "You're right, it's not good enough. I'll get something else, find something... it's all wrong." He looked around at his room in shame and disgust.

Saina couldn't bear the way her chest felt. She had caused that terrible look on his face. She was the reason he was embarrassed of his beautiful hoard. She had cracked the confidence of a man as good as he was gorgeous.

She reached out to him automatically and put a hand on his arm. The touch was electric. "I love the hoard," she said. "It's the most gorgeous hoard I've ever seen. But you can't give it to me, not any of it. Not to me."

"There is no one else in the world for me," Bastian assured her, putting the necklace aside.

Saina felt saltwater in her eyes unexpectedly.

She'd heard plenty of professions of devotion before, been at the receiving end of adoring acts of compelled generosity, but this was the first time she had gone so far as to make someone *love* her before, let alone think she was their mate.

Worse, this was the first time she wanted it to be *real*.

While she struggled to regain her composure, Bastian gathered her up in her arms and kissed her.

Chapter 16

Bastian couldn't disbelieve Saina when she said she loved his hoard. There was no falsifying the admiration in her eyes, no way that her words could have been lies.

She didn't want it, which confused both Bastian and his dragon, but perhaps they'd only chosen the wrong piece; his treasure sense was haywire and he doubted his own understanding of value.

But she wanted *him*.

He knew it in the way she kissed him, and the way she looked at him when she thought he didn't notice.

It wasn't her practiced smiles or her careful eyelashes, it was the other look — the puzzled, tender look she had when she thought he wasn't looking. The crooked smile when something truly amused her. The way she hummed happily to herself when she liked something.

That was the Saina he kissed.

And to his heartbreak, she still pulled away. "I... I can't do this," she said.

"We can take it as slow as you want," he assured her, letting her retreat.

"Oh, Bastian, you deserve so much better than this."

There were tears in her green eyes.

"I'm not your mate, Bastian. Sirens don't *have* mates. It's just my magic, you only think you feel this way, and when I leave, you..." she gave a little sob. "You'll look back at these few days and it will feel like a dream, because that's all it is. It's just a happy little fantasy that I *never* should have indulged in. I'm so sorry. There isn't anything here, between us. It's not... real. It never was."

She turned and fled through the door, and Bastian let her go, too baffled to stop her.

After a moment, he left his lackluster hoard, locking the door behind him.

He walked to the pool deck in a daze, and stared at the "Lifeguard Off Duty" sign for a long, confused moment. He almost took it down, then reconsidered, and realized what he had to do.

Tex called down to him from the bar deck above, but Bastian ignored the bartender and stalked to the beach, not pausing at the little beach bar or the lifeguard tower. He walked straight into the water, shifted, and swam out the same way that he'd gone the day before.

It took several hours of swimming to reach the spot he'd found Saina. There were no features above the waves once the island was out of sight, but beneath the water, he could follow the landmarks of the ocean floor, and if he concentrated very carefully, he could feel a faint tingle of his treasure sense, leading him back to her sunken luggage.

While he swam, he tried to sort out his confused feelings. Saina was his mate. She was his everything. It didn't matter what she said, he knew to the core of his heart that she was his, meant for him in every way.

He loved the charm she could easily turn on, and the vulnerable confusion she so rarely let him see. He loved the way she moved, and the way she swam.

He missed the way she let him breathe underwater and surfaced to suck in a breath of air. The ocean looked like a different place today, smooth and sparkling cheerfully. It wanted to play, today.

He dived again. The ocean floor was hundreds of meters down here; his chest protested the pressure and his tail ached with the effort. It was dark, too, but between his luminous eyes and the faint tug of the treasure sense, he knew he could find his target.

Confidence swelled in him again, tingling through his limbs as he approached the treasure.

She was wrong, he thought, with increasing resolution. He wasn't under her spell. He was too strong and powerful a dragon to be caught in any web of enchantment.

He was too magnificent to be snared by magic, he thought as his treasure sense flared and began to burn with more intensity than it had except for the time he had found Saina.

He was stronger than any siren, his will was harder.

There must be some other reason she was refusing his hoard, but it was of no consequence. He was a dragon, and she was his mate. He would make her the prize of his nest; she would be his finest treasure. There would be no more running from him.

If he had the air to spare, he would have roared, because there, half-buried in shifting sand, was Saina's suitcase, its lurid color washed away by the murkiness of the depths.

He put a claw around the handle and kicked off from the floor of the ocean, making a swift, determined beeline for the surface.

He was not built for water liftoffs; he needed to kick off with his strong hindlegs from something solid to get enough lift to get him into the air, but knowing that he'd never been able to before didn't stop Bastian from believing he could now as a strange resolution crept over him.

He darted for the surface, and just as he broke through it, spread his wings and gave a tremendously powerful beat that took him into the air.

A triumphant laugh turned into a roar of celebratory fire as he escaped the distasteful draw of the saltwater and returned to the air where he belonged, his prize safe in his claws.

He soared through the salty air, snapping at seabirds who dared get in his way, and flew back to Shifting Sands with sure, strong wing strokes.

He circled the resort twice, gratified when the people sunbathing below looked up to admire his big, gleaming body. Then he landed at the back entrance to the kitchen, closest to where he sensed his mate.

Saina! he roared, calling her.

Saina! I have your tribute! You will be mine!

Obediently, as she should, Saina came to the door, Breck and Chef right behind her, staring curiously. Chef was holding a wicked knife, and Breck had a dish towel. Neither of them was any threat.

Bastian dropped the sodden suitcase at his mate's feet. *I have won you*, he snarled.

Her spoken voice was sharp and unexpectedly clear. "You have done nothing of the sort, you idiot."

He opened his jaws and roared flame into the air.

Chapter 17

CHEF PROVED TO BE A large older man with a twinkle in his bright eyes, a white mustache, and biceps the size of winebarrels. He welcomed Saina into his kitchen domain with the open-hearted kindness that she was beginning to accept was a genuine part of this odd resort and showed her the tasks that needed attention.

"Are you sure you are up to this?" he asked sincerely.

Saina rolled her shoulder, turning her head to look at the fading puckered scab. "It's almost all healed," she promised before diving into a soapy sink of dirty dishes.

He continued to regularly check in with her as he moved around the kitchen with busy authority, praising her attention to detail and generally encouraging her in an unexpected way. He sang as he worked, and it was surprising to Saina because it was without method or motive, just for the joy of it.

She joined him, because his pleasure in it was so addictive. She was careful to keep her magic dampened, and to keep her grief from coloring the counterparts she sang. It helped that Chef seemed to like happier tunes, skipping from Italian arias to folk songs as the mood struck him. Most of them weren't songs that Saina knew, but she could improvise a harmony to almost anything, and after a few choruses could usually pick up on lyrics. Breck joined them for a few lines, as he moved in and out of the kitchen bussing tables and restocking and refreshing the buffet.

She was chopping tomatoes for that night's dinner, singing the soprano to "Tonight" from West Side Story and forgetting for a while that she would be leaving very soon, when Bastian broke through her reverie.

Saina! He called her. *Saina! I have your tribute! You will be mine!*

Saina dropped the knife, snatching her hands out of the way in time to avoid disaster, and left it on the counter to answer the call. Judging by the way that Chef and Breck also startled, they'd heard Bastian's imperious words, or perhaps just his roar, and they were at her heels when she came out of the back kitchen door to find a gigantic green dragon perched at the retaining wall.

Her pink rolling carry-on case fell with a sodden thump at her feet.

I have won you, Bastian said, and his golden eyes were shot with glowing red.

Goldshot.

"You have done nothing of the sort, you idiot," Saina could not stop herself from saying, and she saw Bastian flinch and then rear his head back in anger to flame into the air.

She recognized his irrational anger and the unnatural glow to his eyes and scales. She didn't for a moment fear for her own self, but she knew that Bastian would lose his real self if she didn't do anything, and she cast desperately for something she could do to free him as she opened her mouth.

Her grandmother's words came back to her, and she drew power not from her belly, but from her heart. She focused all of her unpredictable magic into the idea of leaching the personality-altering drug from his system. She had to draw out the poison, sing it from his very veins. Not sure it would work, she poured her magic into her song.

Let it go,

Let it die,

Let it out,

Let it fly...

When the last note died away, Saina waited to see if it had worked.

Bastian remained perched on the retaining wall, swaying slightly, and she panted, every muscle in her body aching from the effort.

Chef and Breck looked from one of them to the other, baffled.

Bastian shook his big head and just as Saina was drawing in breath to try another song, he blinked and the remaining red in his eyes faded away. He seemed to draw into himself, suddenly much smaller and less glittery, but there was only a brief moment to observe his dragon before he shifted into a man. Then he was Bastian, vaulting down from the retaining wall to kneel at her feet.

"Saina," he said. "I... don't understand what happened. I'm so sorry."

"You should be," Saina said furiously. "You don't own me and you never will, but more than that, you are an utter fool."

He looked up at her in consternation.

"Do you have any idea what is in that suitcase?" she demanded.

He started to reach for it, and she quickly said, "No, don't touch it!" She crouched next to it and unzipped it, flinging the lid back to reveal a sodden, dissolved gray mass in a slurry of half-empty plastic wrappers. "This is goldshot."

Bastian, poor sweet, innocent Bastian, looked across the luggage at her with no understanding at all.

"Goldshot is what got that French dragon eliminated from the World Mr. Shifter contest," Breck supplied, snapping his fingers with the memory.

"It's a drug," Saina added. "A terrible, expensive designer drug that only works on dragons. You probably absorbed several doses of it getting that close to the stuff dissolving underwater."

"I was a real dragon," he said achingly, standing up and wrapping arms around himself. "For a little while I was a *real* dragon. A dragon of *fire* and *strength*."

"You *are* a real dragon," Saina told him firmly, standing to face him. "And I love you just the way you are, the way you really are, not the trumped up ball of muscle and ego that the goldshot makes you."

He squinted at her, like he was struggling through the worst hangover of his life. He probably was.

"You love me?" he said plaintively.

Saina sighed. "Yes, dammit." It hurt to admit, and felt good at the same time, like pulling off an old scab.

Bastian grinned at her lopsidedly through his pain. "You *are* my mate."

"I'm not," she insisted, but weakly. She wasn't entirely sure of anything anymore. "You shouldn't trust your feelings for me."

"This is not a spell," Bastian insisted. "I know what false confidence feels like now, and that is not what I feel for you."

"I should have brought popcorn," Breck told Chef. "This is better than the Spanish soaps!"

"That's only because you don't speak Spanish," Chef hissed back. "And you're too lazy to read the subtitles."

"What would convince you?" Bastian asked, ignoring them.

His question was meant seriously, Saina realized, he wasn't just speaking metaphorically about having her set an impossible quest for him to complete.

"Time," she said thoughtfully. "Time *away*. My magic wears off if I don't renew it. But..." she swallowed. "I don't trust myself not to cast again, without meaning to. I have never loved anyone before. I don't know how to do it without magic."

Chef and Breck both made suspicious sniffling noises, and Saina glared in their direction.

Chapter 18

BASTIAN WOULD HAVE preferred to have this conversation without an audience, and without a headache so terrible it seemed to sink into his very bones. But fate seemed determined to cross him.

"I was curious as to why I didn't have a lifeguard on duty, and I also believe there were promises about this not happening again if you were to stay here, Saina," a new voice cut in.

Scarlet's arms were crossed and she was standing by the gate to the kitchen garden, looking as if she'd been there for some time.

"The plot thickens," Breck said in a stage-whisper to Chef.

Scarlet turned her icy stare to him. "I believe you have somewhere else to be," she suggested.

Chef helpfully took the head waiter's elbow and dragged him back into the kitchen, shutting the door firmly behind them. Bastian almost laughed, picturing them leaning with their ears against the other side of it. Almost laughing made his head hurt worse.

"I'm sorry," Saina said in small voice.

"It was my fault," Bastian added quickly.

"I'm sure it was," Scarlet said without quarter, looking down at the seeping suitcase. "I want this removed before it gets into the soil," she said in disgust.

75

Bastian automatically bent to pick it up and Saina swiftly said, "No! Don't touch it again!"

She knelt beside the bag and zipped it up, at least slowing the leaks. "I will leave," she said in a small, brave voice. "I am sorry for the trouble I've been."

"No," Bastian said. "You stay here. I have... business I need to attend to." He turned to face Scarlet's wrath. "I need five days off."

Scarlet's face grew chillier. "You realize that we have a new batch of guests and no other lifeguard on staff."

"I can certify Saina," Bastian said swiftly. "Like I did with Neal a few months back. It's just a swimming test I know she can pass, and a few safety and first aid lectures I can pack into an afternoon."

"You don't have to do that," Saina said.

"He might," Scarlet countered dryly.

Bastian turned to Saina. "You told me you need time. Time away from me." The idea of it hurt to his already aching bones. "I'll give you that time."

To Scarlet, he said firmly. "I'm sorry not to give more warning, but this isn't optional."

Scarlet met his gaze without wavering. "How do I know she can control her magic?" she asked, as if Saina wasn't standing right beside them. "I can't have our guests accidentally enspelled because a little girl gets emotional about some setback or imagined slight."

Bastian bristled, wanting to snarl at her for the insult but at the last moment recognized it as bait.

"I can't promise it won't happen again," Saina said calmly in reply. "But I *can* promise that I mean you, your guests, and this place no harm, and I will see that none comes to it while you employ me. I am happy to work here in whatever capacity I can until Bastian returns."

"And then?" Scarlet prodded.

Saina drew in a breath. "I don't know. If he still thinks I'm his mate, I... would like to stay. If he doesn't, you'll be rid of me."

Scarlet considered this for a long moment while Bastian watched Saina's carefully serene face.

"I am satisfied with this," Scarlet finally said. "Bastian, I hope you find what you need. If there is any change to this arrangement, I expect to be notified. I am attempting to run a professional establishment here and I need to be able to rely on my staff."

"Yes, ma'am," he and Saina said together.

Scarlet gave a harrumph in reply and stalked back the way she had come, muttering about dating services and schedules.

Chapter 19

SAINA WATCHED SCARLET go with a sigh of relief. The woman made her uneasy, raising the hair at the back of Saina's neck. The power that seemed to bleed out from her was something she had never felt before and the air was easier to breathe with her gone.

"So, I guess you've volunteered to teach me to be a lifeguard," she said, turning to Bastian. "Can you really do that? Legally, I mean?"

Bastian, still looking like he had a terrific headache, shrugged and gave a lopsided grin. "I'm certified to train lifeguards. I know you can swim, I just have to quiz you on first aid and ocean safety, which I'm also sure you won't have any trouble with, and there's a temporary certificate I sign and a form I mail in to the Civil Guard for the permanent certification."

"Let's go make me a lifeguard," Saina said, and she took Bastian's offered arm and dragged the luggage that had changed her life so drastically behind her.

She dropped the bag at her cottage, wrapped in a garbage bag to keep the ooze from spreading, while Bastian got his lifeguard manuals from his room. They flipped through them together at the pool. "You know CPR?" he asked

"Sure," Saina said.

Bastian flipped a few more pages. "Name the first three things you do with a drowning victim."

"On land or in the water?"

"Assume you've gotten them back to land."

"If they aren't breathing, turn their head to the side so the water drains out, start mouth-to-mouth, and steal their wallet."

Bastian chuckled. "Close enough. Describe two kinds of drowning behavior."

"Well, there's the struggling sort, and the bobbing sort. Plus the being dragged under by tentacles sort, but you hardly ever see that this close to shore."

"What would you do with a hysterical swimmer in the water?"

"Sing them to calmness before I even attempted to get close."

Bastian flipped a few more page. "We can skip that part, then. And the bit about how long you can hold your breath and dive."

"Do we get to practice the mouth-to-mouth?" Saina asked, feeling suddenly mischievous.

She regretted the joke as tasteless as Bastian looked up too quickly and then winced as his head caught up with the motion.

"You need an aspirin," Saina told him.

"About seven of them," Bastian agreed. "But let's get this finished."

Together, they flipped through the rest of the manual, and Saina convinced him that she knew the material well enough.

She demonstrated basic swimming strokes in the pool and showed him rescue carries with a floating mattress.

"You're qualified," Bastian said at last, closing the book and flinching at the sound of it. "I'll sign for it."

Saina dried herself off with one of the fluffy pool towels and frowned at him.

"Let's go get you that aspirin," she said.

She led him down the path to the staff house, where the sign on the door had been further annotated "House of Hooligans" and "Stud House." Both were crossed out.

By the time Saina got Bastian up the stairs, he was staggering badly.

"You poor thing," she said as he fumbled with the lock. "Let's get you into bed."

"I like that idea," he said in a low rumble.

Saina paused in the doorway. "I... I can help you," she offered. "But only if you want me to."

"How do you mean?" Bastian asked sensibly.

"I can rub your shoulders," Saina said hesitantly. Could she really do that without wanting to touch more? "And I can try to sing more of the goldshot from you."

"I'd like that," Bastian said gravely.

Saina made him take four aspirin with an entire glass of water, drew him down onto the bed and kissed his forehead, then took his shirt off carefully.

It was hard not to linger over the muscles of his arms, she wanted nothing more than to kiss down his chest, but Saina made herself stay to her goal. She sat chastely behind him on the bed and began kneading the knots from his shoulders and neck.

He groaned in pleasure as Saina found all the tightest places and applied siren-strong fingers to unwinding them. She hummed as she worked, cautiously letting her magic loosen all the tension from his body and leach what she could of the remaining poison from his blood.

When she was done, he turned abruptly and gathered her into his arms.

"You're supposed to be relaxed now," Saina protested with a squeak.

"You missed a spot," Bastian murmured near her ear. "But my headache is gone."

Saina could not keep her hands from continuing to stroke the tanned lines of his shoulders. "What if... what if you're wrong?" she asked quietly. "What if this is just enchantment, like I said?" She didn't want to stop touching him, she wanted his skin against every inch of hers. It didn't feel like song-fantasy. It was so beautiful and right-feeling, just being with him, held in his strong arms.

Bastian put a hand at her chin and gently tipped her head back so he could look into her eyes. His eyes were all gold now, glimmering like distant treasure. "I will take a moment of enchantment with you over a lifetime without you."

But it wasn't her magic looking back at her, it was Bastian. Not Bastian-on-goldshot, not Bastian-entwined-in-her-spell, just Bastian.

Bastian, who loved her without magic.

Bastian, who wanted her as much as she wanted him.

Saina opened her mouth, and it wasn't to sing.

Chapter 20

BASTIAN HADN'T BEEN honest about his headache; it still lurked behind his eyes and in the pit of his stomach.

But it was nothing compared to the joy of having his love in his arms, her sea green eyes tender and her fingers lithe and clever over his skin.

When he kissed her, he forgot the pain in his head and the hunger in his belly, happy to lose himself in the taste and feel of her against him.

Her dress slipped easily off over her head, his shorts followed swiftly, and for a long, delicious time, they simply touched each other, hands over exposed flesh.

Bastian didn't want to rush her, and held himself to worshipping each plane and curve of her body. He kissed and sucked and nibbled. She did the same in return, cautiously, then eagerly. Mutual fingers traced every sensitive place, looking for the spot that drew the hiss of breath and flush. Her hair tickled him as she kissed his chest and cupped his ass. He licked her neck and traced the small of her back.

Breath grew ragged and Bastian couldn't tell where hers began and his ended; he wondered if her magic would help him breathe without air out of the water as well as it did under it.

Urgency mounted, and the touches grew more intimate; he slipped a questing finger into her wet entrance and kissed her neck as she arched into him. She put her fingers around his eager cock and stroked him until he was ready to cry out loud.

He lay her back on the pillows, loving the dark hair spread on his pillows as it took a hundred hues from the gleaming sea glass he had called treasure before he'd known his true prize.

He slipped into her slowly, with the same deliberate care he had explored her body, and she moaned in pleasure as she spread her legs in welcome.

Bastian was careful, gentle, pausing when she tensed, and she made a little noise of need and pressed herself onto him in a rush.

She was his shield, his holt, he thought. Being deep inside her was the safest place he could imagine.

For a moment, an ugly, unwelcome need interrupted, urging him to be the dragon he'd been so briefly again.

Then Saina cried out as the muscles in her body clenched in orgasm, and that need was forgotten, washed away in cleaner desires.

He returned to his mate, not ready to sate himself and end their bliss, and let her pleasure wash away in a slow, controlled wave.

When she returned to herself, they rolled across the bed so that she was straddling him, and she moved with the same slow, deliberate strokes, drawing him deeper, and deeper, like they were swimming together on a fathomless ocean floor. His senses constricted; he was pressure and slick skin against hot velvet. Her touch, her little sounds of joy, were all that anchored him.

He was ocean and fire, she was the tide and the fuel. They moved in perfect symmetry and as she cried again in release, he lost himself in the only magic he needed from her.

Chapter 21

AFTER BRINGING HER to unknown heights of delight, Bastian collapsed next to her, and Saina didn't have the breath left to hum him to the sleep she knew he needed after his exposure to the goldshot.

She was glad that by the time she had gathered herself, she didn't have to do anything. He was asleep, one strong arm splayed over her belly possessively.

Saina closed her eyes and enjoyed the moment as long as she was able to.

Then, unbidden, doubts crept back.

Had she sung out in the moment of her pleasure? Had she unknowingly cast another seduction spell? Had she been wrong about Bastian's love being untainted of her magic, sure of what she saw because she wanted it so badly?

No, she was sure there had been no enchantment left, but what if distance dampened his ardor and he came back from his trip and looked at her without that same affection?

Saina's chest hurt worse than her shoulder ever had.

She could imagine nothing worse than Bastian looking at her with indifference. The idea of it staggered her, and filled her with fear.

It would be better not to know, to hold this one perfect memory and flee, she realized, looking up at the sea glass glittering over the ceiling. She could be gone before he returned, and she would never have to face that possibility. And she still needed to figure out a way to free her Voice, something she could not do in the safe haven of this resort.

She slipped out from under his arm and wriggled back into her clothing. He was so beautiful, sprawled on his big bed, looking innocent and exhausted in sleep.

Before she left, she circled the room, dragging fingers over the beautiful things he had collected from the ocean she loved. She made the sea glass chime and considered taking just a piece of it, to remember him forever. She paused at the necklace he had tried to give her, so out of place and awkward in his beautiful collection. He had, technically given it to her, but she knew that it had been under false pretense, still thinking she was his mate.

Sirens don't have mates, she reminded herself.

Even if he loved her, some day his true mate would come into his life and he would know that the gift had been an error. She would leave this, even if she disagreed that it was the most valuable part of his hoard.

Would his real mate think so? Would she know how perfect his unusual hoard was, or appreciate the beauty of it?

She supposed the hypothetical partner would have to, if mates were really as perfect as advertised.

She ached at the idea of someone else bringing Bastian joy, but sadly realized that she would rather he was truly happy with someone else than falsely happy with her.

The sun outside the open windows was beginning to plunge to the ocean, turning the sky golden and bleaching the green and blue from the sea glass glinting in the window.

Saina put fingers to a particularly fine piece of glass, a shard as big as her palm that was swirled green and blue and ground by sand and salt to a soft-edged plate. Then she pulled her hand back. She couldn't disturb his hoard.

She had memories to take with her; that was enough.

She crept down the stairs as quietly as she could, hoping to leave unnoticed, but she was greeted at the bottom by Travis, who was just coming up. "Hi, Saina," he said cheerfully, as casually as if she lived there and was already an established part of the staff. "How's the shoulder?"

"All better," she said in surprise. She hadn't thought about it all day.

"I hear you're going to be our lifeguard while Bastian's gone a few days," he continued, friendly.

Saina nodded slowly, surprised by how fast the news had traveled. "I am," she said. And she'd be gone before he returned, she reminded herself.

"Let us know if you need anything," Travis continued, then he was moving past her up the stairs.

It was odd, being the object of friendliness with absolutely no sexual expectations behind it. They accepted her as Bastian's mate, not as something potentially their own.

Even Graham the landscaper, who hadn't said so much as a word to her the few times they had crossed paths, gave a nearly friendly nod from the common room as Saina passed it to get to the door.

She would miss this place, she realized as she shut the door behind her.

Not just Bastian, who was going to leave a hole in the heart she had never believed she had, but the resort had grown on her as well. Her magic felt odd here, but she liked the quirky, big-hearted staff. She even thought Jenny might even become a good girlfriend, something she had never enjoyed before.

She looked out over the cliffs at the rosy-colored ocean.

How completely unexpected.

Chapter 22

BASTIAN WOKE JUST BEFORE the sunrise, knowing at once that something was missing from his hoard.

A thread of anger and hunger rose in the back of his throat before he recognized that Saina was gone. He could still taste her in his mouth, but the bed was cool beside him.

The headache was gone, but the desire remained. He wanted badly to be back the way he'd been with the drug coursing through his veins. He struggled, hating how he'd been to Saina, but loving how simple and powerful it had been to be a complete dragon, strong and sure and single-minded.

Bastian-with-goldshot had known who he was, and where he belonged. He could do anything, stronger and faster than Bastian-without. Bastian-without was adrift, caught between two worlds, unsure of his path.

Bastian-without rubbed his eyes and rolled from the bed.

For the first time in a very long time, he did not dress in his lifeguard uniform, regretfully putting it aside for a light silk shirt from the back of his closet and a pair of tailored gray slacks. Tooled leather shoes were dredged from beneath the bed, and a fine wool suit jacket went over his shoulders. If he was going to battle, he was going to do it well-armored.

It was odd to turn from the staff house door to walk towards the cliffs instead of towards the heart of the resort. He shifted and fell from the cliffs to spread wings and catch the wind in his dragon form.

He felt small and fragile, compared to Bastion-with.

Then he thought of Saina, and his wing beats steadied. Whatever kind of dragon or perversion of dragon he was, he would earn his mate. He had none of her doubts regarding the truth of their bond, but he knew he had one more thing to do before he could completely claim her.

He flew through the sunrise, and through most of the day, following the coast of the mainland Costa Rica. He might have enjoyed the flight, and the pods of dolphins and whales he passed, but he dreaded his destination.

Midafternoon, he arrived, turning inland at the end to climb into the coastal mountains. The compound he arrived at was castle-like in its grandness, with towers intended to imply the royalty he knew his family craved.

He circled the structure once before landing in the secondary courtyard, folding glinting green wings back neatly as he set claw to the stone he thought he'd left behind forever.

He was not surprised when a second dragon, darker green, back-winged into the courtyard moments after.

Mother and Father have no desire to see you, the newcomer said in his silky mind-voice. *You are no longer family, brother-not.*

I didn't come to see them, Bastian replied evenly. *I came for you, Keylor.* He was concerned to see that Keylor seemed significantly larger than he had been mere years ago. Bastian had always been the big brother in both years and mass, but that was no longer the case.

What do you want with me? Keylor sniffed.

I am here to treat with you, Bastian said, drawing himself up to his full height. *I'm here for Saina's Voice.*

Chapter 23

SAINA'S FIRST STINT as lifeguard went smoothly. Bastian's uniform didn't come close to fitting her, but Scarlet provided a staff polo shirt in her size and a pair of nondescript shorts. With the orange high visibility first aid kit strapped at her waist, Saina looked the part, and the swimmers accepted her authority without question.

She found the work easy and enjoyable, bantering with older women on the pool deck who reminded her achingly of her Voice and showing a pair of younger men the basics of the paddle boards at the beach. She reminded pale-skinned people to reapply sunscreen at appropriate intervals, and handed out cold bottles of water and sunhats to guests who weren't used to the intensity of the heat in the tropics.

When the sun began to set and people abandoned both pool and beach, she wasn't sure what to do with herself. After she put all the beach chairs back at the beach bar structure and straightened the now-abandoned pool deck, she wandered up to the bar.

Jenny was sitting at the bar, holding hands with a bartender in a cowboy hat, which puzzled Saina until she realized it wasn't Jenny, just a woman who looked exactly like her.

"I'm Laura," she said, offering a hand as Saina approached the bar. "You met my identical twin sister, Jenny."

"Saina," she answered, accepting the hand for a polite shake.

"You're looking considerably better than the last time I saw you here," Laura teased gently.

Saina realized that Laura must have been present when Bastian brought her to the resort. "Well," she said dryly, "I imagine it's not too hard a bar to beat, given that I was bleeding all over the place at the time."

Laura laughed.

"What can I get you?" the bartender asked, after introducing himself aptly as Tex.

"Is staff supposed to drink here?" Saina asked cautiously.

"As long as you don't make a habit of getting falling down drunk on the expensive stuff or get in the way of serving the guests, Scarlet gives us free rein and encourages us to eat and drink well," Tex said. "The profit shares have been pretty nonexistent, so she wants the room and board to be a fair trade for our work."

"Seems like a sweet deal," Saina said wistfully. It was getting harder and harder to think about turning her back on the resort. "Can I have something light and fruity, just a little alcoholic?"

"Yes, ma'am," Tex said, putting his fingers to the brim of his hat.

As he bent to mix her drink, Laura gave her a sidelong look and a grin. "So. Bastian."

Saina was glad her golden-brown skin didn't show a blush easily, and she had to use all of her willpower not to squirm in her seat. How could she explain that she wasn't Bastian's mate, that she'd just enspelled and deluded the poor man and then had the poor grace to fall in love with him? Whether he loved her without magic or not, they were not mates.

She didn't want to talk about Bastian.

"Is that a karaoke machine?" she asked desperately, hoping to deflect the topic.

"It is," Tex said, setting the umbrella-topped drink in front of her. "Care to fire it up? Usually it doesn't see a lot of use until the evening drinking crowd really settles in."

Most of the guests were on the deck above, eating Chef's fine food at the gourmet restaurant, but a few were nursing before-dinner drinks here in the bar, scattered between the tables in the open air bar and out on the uncovered deck, where stars were just beginning to appear in the purple sky.

Saina took a sip of her drink, eyeing the little stage hesitantly.

"I'm dying to hear you sing," Laura admitted. "Jenny says you have the most gorgeous voice."

Saina gave her a hard look, trying to determine if she'd heard about the things Saina could do with her voice, or if it was an innocent request.

The mischievous look on her face suggested it was not innocent.

Saina's eyes narrowed. She wondered if Laura would prove as impossible to enchant as Jenny had.

"Of course, I could quiz you about Bastian, instead," Laura suggested breezily.

"Hush, love," Tex chided her. "It's not always easy at first, and we should know. Give her space and let her enjoy her drink."

Laura pouted good-naturedly.

Saina was puzzled. This wasn't the mean-spirited kind of teasing she was used to in the siren pod. They were smiling, not only at each other, but inclusively at her. They would give her space if she asked for it, and she thought that they would be willing and understanding ears if she wanted to talk about Bastian. She wondered what they could tell her about him, and then remembered that she was planning to leave before he came home. She didn't need to know more about him, as badly as she wanted to.

Suddenly singing seemed like the much simpler choice.

Chapter 24

KEYLOR SLITHERED TO one side, flaring his wings. *So, you've met Saina the siren. Did she enchant you into coming to fight for her?*

I am not enspelled, Bastian said, calmly confident. He remained seated, wings neatly at his back, not returning Keylor's posturing. *You have done her family wrong*, he said reproachfully.

Is that what she told you? Keylor scoffed, drawing himself up. *Made herself out to be the innocent victim of a cruel dragon deal?*

Bastian reminded himself not to rise to Keylor's baiting. *If there is a debt, let me pay it and call it done. Release her Voice!*

Slights of honor cannot be repaid with gold. At least not the amount of gold in your ridiculous hoard.

Bastian chewed on this.

Sirens lie, Keylor told him. *They thrive on power and control. They backstab and weave fantasies as a matter of nature.* He paused, and gave Bastian a sly sideways look. *If she said she loved you, it was a falsehood.*

Bastian wanted to mantle his wings and hiss fire at the idea that Saina's love was untrue, but he kept himself controlled.

Oh, brother-not, do you really believe you love her? You are a bigger fool than I ever knew.

This is not about me, Bastian snarled. *This is about releasing her Voice.*

Her Voice is mine now. She has a debt to repay and I do not choose to release it. I gave Saina a chance to buy it out, but she must have failed, if you are here now.

Then I challenge you for that contract, Bastian said.

Keylor laughed derisively. He spread his wings and drew himself up, demonstrating beyond a shadow of a doubt that he was indeed larger than Bastian now, and his scales had a deep, healthy glimmer to them that suggested greater strength. *You think you have a chance against me?*

Bastian was privately thinking he probably didn't, but he wasn't about to admit this, keeping his head high and proud.

Then he realized that Keylor's eyes, which had always been the same golden as Bastian's, were glowing red. As he furrowed his dragon brow, his human realized, *Goldshot!* Keylor was dosing on goldshot. Pieces of the puzzle fell into space. Keylor had sent Saina to get more of the drug, not for its street value, but for *himself.*

If Bastian had goldshot himself, he would be even mightier, he thought grimly. He would be stronger, faster...

I accept your challenge, Keylor roared, and he pounced, claws outstretched.

Chapter 25

SAINA TOOK ONE LAST sip of her drink and then stood, leaving the lifeguard first aid kit behind her on the counter.

The karaoke machine had the usual selection; mostly pop music and classic rock.

Saina picked a love song at random and settled herself behind the microphone as the opening bars of music played.

The first line, she kept her magic dampened, relying only on the clear sound of her voice to set the emotional tone.

That got some of the attention in the bar, a few people turning their chairs so they could watch her. She knew she wouldn't be as eye-catching as she usually was, in her understated staff polo shirt and unremarkable shorts, but she stood as tall and confidently as if she were wearing an evening gown and when the chorus came around, she leaned into the song.

You are my star
However far
I will wish on you
I will always miss you...

She hadn't intended to pick a song with a sad undertone, but when she heard her own voice singing the words, she could only think of Bastian, and how she would never see him again.

By the second round of the chorus, everyone in the bar was completely enraptured, and drinks were forgotten on their tables.

Saina could feel power resonate deep beneath her, like the resort itself was on a pocket of magic that was leaking out of a dozen cracks in the earth. She could tap it, she realized. She could rule this place, she thought, giddy with the strength of it. She could worm her way into every heart and force them to love her; it could drown out the gaping place that Bastian would leave.

She reached out with her voice, held their hearts, and squeezed.

The urge was like a whisper in her ear, tickling at the back of her mind.

She was a siren and they would obey her.

They were hers, all hers, and she could force them to feel anything she wanted. And with this army of shifters to command, no one could keep her from her goals.

She poured her agony and loss into the last stanza, then suddenly thought, *Bastian wouldn't want this.*

She remembered his quiet confession that he had wanted to save people and heal them, despite coming from a family of warriors.

She didn't have to be like other sirens, either, always seeking control and self-satisfaction.

She looked out over the audience, their tear-streaked cheeks and agonized expressions, and she let the last note release them, holding it while she keyed up the next song, a cheerful pop song that swiftly devolved into happy nonsense.

Instead of reaching down to the great pools of magic below, Saina let it lie, and kept her spell light and easy, an invitation, not a command. Be happy, she suggested with it. Be joyful and love each other.

Bastian would have wanted that.

These were his people, his place. As badly as she wanted for it to be her own, it was his. She didn't know where she fit in the world without him, but it wasn't here, knowing she wasn't wholly his. And it certainly wasn't at the head of a shifter army. Where had such an idea even come from? She had no desire for that kind of power and control. If that made her a poor excuse of a siren, she could accept that.

Chapter 26

BASTIAN AND KEYLOR battled as only dragons can, claws drawing along hardened scales, fire singeing, crashing into courtyard walls and stair railings as they beat wings at each other and slashed with tails at sensitive eyes and undersides.

Keylor was stronger, longer-limbed, and faster.

But Bastian was smarter, and he had unexpected endurance from his years of diving.

He could hold his breath when Keylor ignited the air around him, when Keylor had to suck hot breath in, and stagger back as the heat scorched unprotected throat and lungs, or pull his head back out of the flame, leaving himself exposed to slashing claws and gnashing teeth.

They tumbled, wings tangling, and tore scales from each other.

Keylor fought like a thing possessed, confident in his superior strength.

Bastian fought like he swam, making the best use of his advantages and compensating for his weaknesses.

He also had more to lose; if he lost this challenge, he knew he would lose Saina's Voice, and with her, Saina.

So he poured everything into his fight, ignoring the bites and the wing tears when it allowed him to slip past Keylor's defenses.

When Keylor leaped onto one of the walls, trying to increase his advantage with height, Bastian gathered himself and leaped after him, and Keylor took the battle to the air with strong wing beats.

Come and get me brother-not, he taunted.

This was a new disadvantage for Bastian, whose strength was not so concentrated in his wings. They swept upwards, then tumbled and dove, slashing and flaming at each other

Bastian tried to use fast, sniping techniques, only to find that Keylor was faster, and still stronger, and met every attack with confidence and cunning.

They battered at each other, angry and mighty, and red blood stained green scales as they fought.

Bastian wanted to protest that this was not an honorable fight; they would be evenly matched if Keylor were not dosed with goldshot. Or, he thought lustfully, if he were also dosed.

I concede! he finally said when they broke apart at last. Fair or not, this would be Keylor's fight. Bastian had failed Saina.

Keylor paused to pose with an egotistical roar. *Win! Smite! Flame!*

I conceded! Bastian protested, darting aside at the last moment as Keylor shot a column of flame where he'd been.

Fight! Kill! Dominate! Keylor's eyes were brilliant red, glowing in madness and bloodlust.

Stop! Brother! Bastian had to dive aside as Keylor came for him, claws-first. He rolled barely in time, and claws scraped across hard scales.

Brother-not! Keylor replied derisively, flaming in his direction.

Bastian began to concentrate on escape, winging upwards while holding his breath. Keylor caught him easily, wings more powerful and more used to flying. Bastian bit and flamed, then darted away through the clouds, trusting his nose.

Keylor was not going let his prey go willingly now; he was out for blood, not just victory.

Bastian desperately winged through the low coastal clouds, twisting away from Keylor's teeth and claws, slashing with his tail as he climbed into the sky and dived away. Only the fact that he wasn't flying in a predictable dragon pattern kept him safely ahead of the glinting weaponry... and it didn't last long.

Prey! Claw! Kill! Keylor slashed him with a swipe of a lucky claw at his underbelly, and when Bastian's wing beats faltered in pain and shock, Keylor caught him with his tail, and put claws to his chest as his own strong wings kept them aloft.

There is no honor in this, Bastian roared, flaming directly into Keylor's face to drive him back.

Honor is a dead thing, Keylor replied, and he flexed his claws into Bastian's chest, piercing the finer scales around his heart.

Chapter 27

SAINA SANG THE LAST bars without the slightest hint of magic, and the bar broke into applause.

Above them, the restaurant, which had frozen to listen, also cheered, and there were even whistles and stomps. Saina replaced the microphone and stepped down from the little stage, and everyone went cheerfully back to their meals and drinks, exactly as she'd meant them to.

Tex and Laura, however, stared at her when she returned to the bar.

"That was... interesting," Tex said diplomatically.

"Beautiful," Laura was quick to add. "You do have a gorgeous voice."

"Yes, ma'am," Tex agreed.

"But I thought I was going to enlist in some crazy zombie army for a few moments there," Laura confessed.

Saina looked at her in consternation. She shouldn't *remember* that fleeting compulsion.

She looked over at Tex thoughtfully. They both looked rattled, but not... enchanted.

"I wonder if it is because you are mates," Saina said suddenly. "Most people don't have clear memory of siren manipulation."

Tex and Laura looked at each other and shrugged in unison. Their connection was so tangible and beautiful. Saina allowed herself a pang of envy. That was what Bastian thought they had. It was a more lovely fantasy than anything she could have woven for him.

To her surprise, they did not seem to be afraid of her after that. Tex handed her drink back across the bar, and Laura gave her a twinkling smile and went to take drink orders from the newcomers to the bar, and do a quick round to make sure everyone else was still satisfied. A pair of giggly girls took the karaoke stage after her, teasing each other as they made their song selection from the menu.

"Saina?"

Saina froze at Scarlet's familiar voice and turned slowly to face her.

Scarlet looked no more enchanted than Tex and Laura had. Did she have a mate, too? She looked more put together than she had the last time they'd met, her bright hair pulled tightly back without a single strand escaping.

"Yes, ma'am?" Saina said with a crooked smile, trying to look brave.

"A word, if you don't mind." Scarlet did not wait for her response, but turned and clicked away with her sensible business shoes into the darkness past the bar deck to the stairs down to the pool deck. Saina scrambled after her, feeling shabby and chastised in her cheap flip-flops.

At the bottom of the steps, Scarlet continued down the pool deck, pausing only to pick up a towel that Saina had missed, draped at the foot of one of the lounge chairs.

At the dark end of the pool, where the deck wrapped around to overlook the beach, she finally stopped so that Saina could catch up with her. The chatter from the bar and restaurant faded to a hum and the chorus of night frogs and insects made a pleasant drone against the waves lapping the beach below.

"That was an impressive show," Scarlet said, her voice carefully neutral.

"It wasn't what I... expected," Saina said honestly in return.

How much did the resort owner know about the pool of power underneath the resort, Saina wondered.

"You showed... restraint."

Well, she knew something, then.

Saina lifted her chin in challenge. "I'm a siren," she told Scarlet frankly. "Restraint may not be something we're known for, but I promised no harm to your resort."

Scarlet smiled in the faint light. "I'm pleased to see that you recognize the gravity of a contract," she said. Then, unexpectedly, "I was impressed with your performance as a lifeguard today, but I was perhaps unnecessarily dismissive when you told me you were a performer earlier. If you choose to stay here at Shifting Sands, I would be pleased to put you on our entertainment schedule."

Saina suspected that was as close to an apology as Scarlet would get, and it was gracious. She was touched. "I would love that," she said in an uncharacteristic rush — then she remembered that she would be leaving in a few days and the familiar pang of regret squeezed her chest. "But I... won't be staying."

Scarlet's expression was not surprised. "You plan to leave before Bastian returns," she said dryly.

Saina pursed her lips, not exactly answering. "He's not my mate. And I have unfinished business to take care of. I don't mean to waste your time."

"I have no patience for drama," Scarlet warned her.

"Yes, ma'am," Saina started to say, then she staggered in place, clutching her chest and gasping for air.

Everything was black pain, then Saina was aware that Scarlet had her by the arm, looking her anxiously in the face.

"Bastian," she choked helplessly. "Bastian, you idiot!"

Chapter 28

BASTIAN FELL, TUMBLING without purpose.

He was distantly aware of Keylor's roar of triumph above him as he tumbled through the clouds. He'd failed Saina, lost his bid to free her Voice. There was nothing left.

Bastian, you idiot!

Saina's voice flared in his mind, sharp and angry.

I had to try, he told her, apologetically.

You have to come back to me, she said fiercely. *Now!*

Bastian was tired, and fighting with her seemed like more work than twisting, folding his wings against his back and diving into the ocean surface that was rushing up at him. He had, at least, been able to lead their fight out over the water.

As he broke through the waves and was once again cradled in the comfortable saltwater he knew so well, he thought belatedly that he should have brought the fight here, to his own element. Keylor, even with goldshot coursing through his veins, wouldn't have stood a chance against him here.

Air, Bastian. Go up and breathe now. Saina's voice in his head was all that could make him move again, and he obediently broke the surface again, pain blossoming in his chest as he drew in a heavy breath. *What did he do to you?* Bastian couldn't tell what was her agony and what was his.

Kicked my ass, he said. *Sideways.* He had to add defensively, *But only because he was dosed up on goldshot.* Did it sound like an excuse?

I could have told you that he would be, Saina said in exasperation. *Bastian, you have got to tell me your stupid plans beforehand so I can talk you out of them.*

I will, Bastian said meekly.

Go breathe again, Saina chided him. Bastian hadn't even realized he'd gone beneath again, half drifting rather than swimming. Swimming hurt.

He broke the surface too close to a ship. He squinted at it in tired confusion. They wouldn't see him, of course. He was masked in the way that dragons naturally were, and only other mythic shifters would see him in this form.

Slowly, as it bore down on him, he realized it was a container ship, chugging south at a steady clip, faster than he'd be able to swim in his current state. It should pass Shifting Sands in just a day or so. He dove just as it came upon him, and rolled, shuddering at the effort, to come up alongside it, hooking one forearm into the docking clips and letting it drag him forwards.

Clever Bastian, Saina said in his head. *I will come meet you.*

Am I clever, or an idiot? Bastian found the energy to tease, shifting his grip to ease the pain in his chest. *Make up your mind.*

You're both, Saina said. *My dear, clever idiot.*

Chapter 29

"I have to go to him," Saina told Scarlet, as she realized the red-haired woman was still holding her up with one arm. "He's hurt, he needs me."

She could stand again, and Scarlet let go of her carefully.

"Is there anything you need?"

Bastian, Saina thought achingly. *I need Bastian.* She shook her head to clear it, and Scarlet took it as an answer.

Scarlet sighed. "Our boat has not been replaced or I would offer you the use of it. Our usual alternative would be to have Bastian himself do an airlift, but that is of course not possible. I could check the guest list and see if we have any other dragons at the resort currently who may be able to take you, but I don't recall any."

Saina suspected that the offer was only a courtesy, that Scarlet had the list memorized. "I will swim," she said firmly. "He has caught a ride on a freighter headed this way, so it won't be long until I can get to him." She looked down at herself. "I should get the first aid kit." She would be able to shift anything she was wearing with her, and it might come in handy. She remembered that it was resort property. "Er, may I borrow it?"

"Yes," Scarlet said promptly. Then she added, "Saina?"

Saina braced herself to meet any argument against her departure.

"We're all very fond of Bastian," the owner said gently. "Bring him back safely."

"I will," Saina promised firmly.

She had to.

Chapter 30

BASTIAN LET THE SHIP drag him in a daze through most of a day, exhausted muscles cramping and wounds stinging from saltwater as they continued to ooze precious blood.

He could dimly hear sailors arguing over the poor performance of the vessel he was clinging to, and knew he must be slowing it considerably.

Saina remained close in his head, teasing him, reminding him to breathe if he let his head slip beneath the surface for too long, even singing to him when the pain grew unbearable.

His strength felt like it was coming to an end when Saina finally told him, *Let go. I'm here.*

He opened gleaming eyes, not even aware that he'd closed them, and groaned, slowly let his cramping forearm release the ship. It was full night, and he could not see her at first, but her hands on his nose let him breathe freely as they sank to the bottom of the ocean.

Saina, he said weakly, drifting down.

My treasure, she said sweetly, her loose hair tickling sensitive scales on his dragon face as she leaned into it with her arms wrapping around him.

They reached the bottom of the ocean with a lazy, gentle landing in soft sand. A stingray that had been hiding there high-tailed away from his monstrous shape.

Bastian drowsed as she swam the length of his body, making angry, concerned noises over the cracked scales and wounds, gentle hands exploring the damage.

You aren't bleeding badly anymore, she said at last.

Just need to rest, heal, Bastian said, fighting to stay conscious. *Sleep.*

You sleep, she said fiercely, laying a kiss on his big head. *I will watch.*

Bastian had never felt safer.

Chapter 31

BASTIAN GROANED AS he settled into the sand, wrapped his tail over his feet, and closed his giant eyes. It was darker with them closed, but Saina was relieved to hear his breathing grow steady as he fell into sleep. She found that he continued to breathe easily as long as she was within arm's length and she inspected the scaled length of him again.

Satisfied that nothing else could be done to make him more comfortable, Saina curled into the hollow by his neck, where his tail made a perfect resting place.

Nothing dared to disturb them, but Saina didn't allow herself to sleep. She did sing, a wordless, watery song of comfort for Bastian, tangled with a warning to anything that might encroach.

As dawn began to send tendrils of color into the dark water, Bastian stirred at last.

I'm here, Saina told him at once, letting her voice rest.

I failed you, Bastian sighed.

That's the first thing you think of? Saina scolded him.

You are the first thing I will always think of, Bastian responded. *And the last thing when I sleep.*

Saina couldn't reply for a long moment, and she suspected that she would have been crying if she hadn't already been cradled in saltwater. *How do you feel?* she was finally able to ask.

113

In answer, Bastian unwrapped his tail and stretched his body, creaking and wincing as he uncoiled. *Better*, he said in surprise. *Better than I expected.*

We're still a ways from Shifting Sands, Saina told him. *Can you make the trip, or is it better to stay here another day?*

Let's go home, Bastian said.

Alright, Saina agreed reluctantly. She would have liked to see Bastian gain more strength first.

They were almost halfway back before Saina recognized that she had unthinkingly accepted Shifting Sands as her own home as well.

They swam at her speed, which would have been ridiculously slow for Bastian at any other time, but it was a terrible effort for him now.

When they reached the reef protecting the beach of Shifting Sands, Saina convinced Bastian to shift to human.

"I'm a lifeguard now," she reminded him. "You should listen to me."

She pulled him gently the rest of the way to shore, using the very carry they had practiced in the pool.

They rose from the surf on the resort beach in human form, Saina wriggling up under his arm so that some of Bastian's exhausted weight was on her as they waded through the waves up onto the sand.

Sunbathing guests greeted them with surprise, and someone offered a bottle of water from the little beach bar. Saina realized that Bastian was dressed in a fine silk suit, absolutely destroyed by blood and saltwater where it hadn't been ripped and torn. His human skin showed bruising that had been masked by his dragon scales.

Tex met them at the bottom of the stairs to the beach and took Bastian's other arm over his own shoulder to help them up the steps.

"His room," Saina gasped. "His hoard will help him heal fastest."

Bastian was staggering and made a noise that might have been protest. He wouldn't want anyone else seeing his hoard, she realized, and then Travis was taking the rest of his weight from her. She fought down a pang of jealousy as the two helped Bastian across the pool deck and up the next flight of stairs.

Scarlet was waiting on the bar deck, but to Saina's relief, only looked concerned, not the slightest bit angry.

The owner did not move to delay them, only surveyed the activity and exchanged a wordless nod of greeting with Saina as they went past. Guests openly stared, and Scarlet walked across the tile to personally reassure them that everything was under control while Tex and Travis manhandled Bastian through the staff door.

Saina wondered what Scarlet would tell their audience.

Laura or Jenny met them there, Saina honestly wasn't sure which. She was wearing the white apron of the spa, her hands still in plastic gloves as protection from whatever she had been working on.

"Is he...?" she asked.

"He's going to be fine," Saina said truthfully. "He just needs to rest and heal up."

There were so many stairs. Narrow steps that the three men didn't even fit on together past the staff gate, broad steps along the main path, then three flights of stairs within the staff house.

Saina didn't pause to find out what house names they were currently considering.

At the door to his room, Bastian gathered himself. "I can do this," he said, shrugging off Travis and Tex and reaching into a battered pocket for his key. Lifting his arms up to the lock made him groan, and Saina took the key from him without protest.

"*I* can do this," she said firmly.

To the other two, she smiled her gratitude. "We've got it from here, boys," she said lightly while Bastian clung to the doorframe. "I can get him into bed."

"No doubts there," Travis said archly.

"Yes, ma'am," Tex said more diplomatically, elbowing Travis in the ribs.

As they turned away and tromped back down the stairs, Saina unlocked the room and helped Bastian limp into the room to fall face forward into his bed.

Chapter 32

BASTIAN SWAM BACK TO consciousness, found blissful contentment in Saina's presence and the harmony of his hoard, and went immediately back to sleep.

The second time he came awake, she was sitting cross-legged on the bed beside him, and he recognized that the smell of the food she was holding was what had woken him.

She smiled when he stirred.

"I thought that something tasty from Chef might coax you back to the waking world," Saina said.

Bastian groaned as he sat up. His wounds had all healed into fresh scars, but he felt very much as if he'd been tenderized by something large and unfriendly.

And he was famished.

Saina fed him the first few bites, and he could feel his energy begin to return, rising with his appetite. It was some sort of creamy, herb-flavored pasta, with thick, homemade noodles.

He took the fork from her and fed himself when she seemed too slow.

"You slept for two days," she told him, handing him a tumbler of cool water to wash it down with. "But you certainly look better for it."

Bastian downed the water and handed the glass back. "I should have known better than to challenge Keylor."

Saina balled up a fist and hit him in the shoulder. "Damn straight."

It didn't hurt as much as Bastian had feared.

"And what was with having a knock-down, dragon-out fight? I thought you dragons just listed your hoards to each other and the winner was the one worth more!"

Bastian snorted. "Maybe that's what those anemic European dragons do, but New World dragons have never had to worry as much about collateral." He looked around his hoard, feeling ashamed. "And I would have lost that fight, anyway."

"Because Keylor has *gold*?" Saina scoffed. She ran her hand along the sea glass that hung above the bed, making it chime. "Your hoard is *tuned*."

She touched a shell nestled in the netting above the headboard. "You have a perfect unbroken ammonoid shell."

She rolled off the bed and danced across the room to the anchor. "This anchor is from the *Morning Star*, lost north of Australia in 1814. The wreck was never found!"

"Keylor wouldn't even know what to do if I started listing these," Bastian laughed. "He'd sprain something laughing."

"His loss," Saina said with a shrug, returning to the bed.

"You are the crown of my fortune," Bastian said, reaching for her.

She came willingly into his arms, tickling his neck with her kiss.

"Do you accept that you are my mate now?" He had to ask.

She drew back and gazed into his eyes. "I don't know about mates," she confessed. "It seems like a far-fetched fairy tale to me. But..." she placed her hand on Bastian's chest. "I cannot deny that you are a part of me. The very best part."

Bastian put hands on either side of her face and kissed her. "My treasure," he said happily.

He kissed her until his muscles ached, then drew back. "What are we going to do about your Voice?" he asked soberly.

Her eyes grew shadowed. "I'll think of something," she vowed. "I have to."

Bastian brushed her hair back from her face. "We'll think of something," he said confidently.

Saina's eyes narrowed thoughtfully. "Your parents, they are very strict, and honorable?"

"There's a reason that draconian is a term for being harsh and exacting," Bastian said dryly. "I think that the only thing my parents value more than honor is the nobility they lack."

"They aren't royalty? I sort of assumed that because of their edict for your return, they were trying to keep their lines clean."

"Rich, of course, but neither has ever really forgiven themselves for their own low origins. I guess they hoped to gain some sort of royal stink for themselves if I married into it."

"Intriguing," Saina said. "But I'm not sure how to work that to our advantage. Now, when you were disgraced, did you forfeit your hoard?"

Bastian gave a dry bark of a laugh. "I would have, but no one wanted it."

"That's more useful," she said thoughtfully.

"What do you have in mind?" Bastian asked suspiciously.

"I'm not sure yet," she said slyly. "But I think we may need Chef's help."

Chapter 33

AFTER ASSURING BASTIAN that he could not help with the first phase of her plan, Saina reluctantly left him. Even with a rainbow of bruises and a crushed ego, he was the most intoxicating man she had ever met. She wondered if he didn't have a little bit of siren in him somewhere, the way he enchanted her.

Chef was on the restaurant deck. It was the end of the breakfast window, and a few guests were lingering, enjoying a last cup of coffee or relishing a last sweet pastry or piece of fruit. Chef often liked to come out at this time, or whenever the kitchen wasn't busy, and mingle with guests. He was a charming mix of friendly and professional, and Saina wondered if he ever broke out in song as he did in the kitchen.

He was standing by the table of one of the largest women that Saina had ever seen.

"I insist you sit," the woman was saying, indicating the opposite chair with an imperious fork. "I cannot make informed decisions with you hovering around like a common servant." Her words were kind, but brooked no argument.

Chef sat, looking unaccountably as if he would prefer to kneel.

Saina tried not to fidget, and Chef caught sight of her over the woman's shoulder.

"Saina," he said, rising again with impeccable politeness. The seated woman gave a noisy sigh. "How is Bastian doing?"

"He's awake," Saina said, moving into the social ring of the table as the woman looked around at her. "Ma'am," she said in polite greeting.

"This is Magnolia," Chef introduced, bowing in her direction.

"And you must be Saina," Magnolia said, giving her an openly appraising look. "I cannot count how many hearts you must have broken by being Bastian's mate."

That was not the fashion in which sirens usually broke hearts. "I... ah, yes, I'm Saina," she said, caught off-guard.

Magnolia offered a hand of round bejeweled fingers to delicately shake. "A delight to meet you. I am looking forward to hearing you sing. I have heard so much!"

That wasn't usually a good thing, Saina thought wryly.

"What can I do for you?" Chef asked. "You look like a woman on a mission."

Saina glanced sideways at Magnolia. "I came to ask for a favor."

Her cautious look did not go unnoticed. "Whatever mischief you are planning, I will find out eventually," Magnolia said arrogantly. "And if you two don't sit, I shall become cross."

Saina and Chef both sat obediently, and Saina gave Magnolia as frank an appraisal as she'd received. Violet eyes looked back from a serene face ending in unabashed extra chins. Gorgeous auburn hair was perfectly styled down past the seat of her groaning chair.

Her gaze was sharp and intelligent, and warm with friendliness.

Finally, Saina smiled. "Here's what I need..."

After Chef approved of her plan, Saina walked down from the restaurant deck past the bar towards her cottage.

She waved at Tex, behind the bar, and Laura, who was clearing tables, and winced at the 'No Lifeguard on Duty' sign beside the pool below. Scarlet hadn't said one word about their delinquency, but Saina knew that this tolerance wouldn't last indefinitely.

As she went to the gate that would take her home, a wild-haired figure stepped in front of her.

"My friend doesn't trust you," the young woman said.

Saina took an automatic step back. "Who is your friend?" she asked in alarm. She had heard of Gizelle, and spotted her several times in her gazelle form from across the lawn, but had never spoken to the shy girl.

Gizelle stood up tall, unexpectedly as tall as Saina, every bone in sharp relief under her pale skin. "I'm friends with the stars in the sky and the sunlight in shadows. But the ocean eats the shore."

Saina started to speak, and fell instead.

She was standing in a strange field, sunlight illuminating grass endlessly in all directions, but when she slowly lifted her head, moving as if she was in an ocean of molasses, the sky above was black and featureless.

She opened her mouth to cry out or sing her way back, and was surprised to find that she was entirely mute. It should have alarmed her, but everything felt impossibly heavy and mean-ingless. She wanted to lie down and sleep, but even that much motion seemed like too much effort.

Then she was blinking in the brilliant tropical sunshine again.

"Gizelle, honey, what are you doing?"

Saina shook her head and staggered a few steps away. She felt drunk and tingly, as if all of her limbs had been asleep. She recognized Tex's voice, and then Laura's.

"Are you alright? Saina?" There was an odd clicking sound, and Saina realized that Laura was snapping her fingers in front of Saina's face.

"I, ah, what happened?"

Gizelle was still looking at her, but from behind a curtain of her salt-and-pepper hair now, a shy smile blooming on her face.

"Gizelle, sweetie, you're not supposed to do that to people," Tex was scolding her gently.

"It's okay," Gizelle told him, cocking her head at him. "I like her now."

Then she was scampering away.

"This is a very strange place," Saina said in confusion.

"You've only seen it on a slow day," Laura said wryly.

Chapter 34

BASTIAN'S HEAD HURT.

The sunset sent stabbing rays of light into his eyes and he squinted at it with a draconic scowl. The last of the beach sunbathers and swimmers were packing up their bags and returning to the resort for their dinners and drinks, and he was glad to see them go.

He shifted to human to collect the chairs and the minor litter they'd left behind. The beach bar was briefly straightened, and Bastian bundled up the trash to take with him. It felt impossibly heavy.

Saina was waiting for him at the top of the beach steps, and his heart lifted.

In the last rays of the sun, she was a dark-haired, golden goddess, all curves and swirls. She took the bag of trash from him and took his hand in her own. Her fingers were strong and his skin against hers was like the touch of a unicorn's horn in tainted water; he could feel the headache ebb away and the black mood that had haunted him faded.

"How are you feeling?" she asked, after she had tossed the trash and helped him pick up all the towels on the pool deck and reorder the chairs.

"Better," Bastian said stoically.

"Liar," Saina scoffed.

"Why'd you ask if you knew the answer?" Bastian sulked. They were standing at the far end of the pool deck, looking out over the dark beach, and he leaned down on the railing.

Saina answered with a kiss on his cheek. "Being grouchy is totally normal for goldshot withdrawal," she said with understanding.

"It's awful," Bastian admitted. "I have never felt so weak and useless and hungry."

"Dinner is being served now, but we could grab something from the staff house or the back of the kitchen."

"That's not the kind of hungry," Bastian complained.

Saina put an arm over his shoulder, pressing herself against his side. "I'm so sorry," she said, leaning her head against him. "This wouldn't have happened if it weren't for me."

"I'm not sorry," Bastian said swiftly. "I mean, this is awful, but I will get over it eventually. I would take this a hundred times over for the chance of meeting you."

"I'm not worth it," Saina said bitterly. "Sirens are never worth their ticket price."

"You are," Bastian told her sincerely. "I would take goldshot hangovers for a century to spend one day with you."

She looked at him in wonder. "You really mean that."

"Dragons are always honest."

"Mermaids never are," she retorted.

"I will always trust you," Bastian said firmly.

"Then you're a fool," Saina said, with her crooked true smile.

Bastian smiled at her, and reached to smooth a lock of hair back from her face. "A glad one."

She kissed him, then, wriggling between him and the railing to put arms around his neck.

Her lips were healing, chasing the last vestiges of pain from his head.

When he drew back for breath, he had to ask, "Are you sure about this plan?"

"I'm only sure of one thing in this world," Saina said gravely. "And that's you."

Chapter 35

SAINA WASN'T SURE HOW this had turned into such a production. The little conference room behind the kitchen was crammed with people and suggestions. Her pink suitcase was open on the table on a plastic trash bag. The goldshot sludge had dried to a brittle crust.

Travis had brought an array of plastering tools and a bucket of gypsum. Chef had bins of flour and sugar.

"I don't want to kill him if he actually takes it," Saina said firmly, looking with question at Travis' bucket. "It just needs to fool him for a little while."

Laura picked up a crust of goldshot with a gloved hand. Jenny, like a double-image beside her, poked a piece with her pen. "Are you sure it's safe to touch?"

"It won't have any effect on you unless you're a dragon," Saina promised.

Jenny's face quirked into a smile. "Well, I don't think so, but I didn't know I was an otter for the longest time, so who knows!" She kept her bare hands well away.

Chef boldly plucked a rind of the substance off and held it up to the light. It had a slight iridescent sparkle to it. "How heavy did you say the cakes were?"

"Maybe 3 kilos apiece," Saina guessed, showing the size with her hands. "Denser than you'd think."

Half the staff looked at her blankly while the others nodded. "A little more than 6 pounds," she added for the Americans and English.

"A quarter of a brick of gold," Breck offered. Saina wasn't even sure why the waiter was there, or how he knew the weight of a brick of gold.

"Fruitcake," Graham suggested dryly. Even the dour landscaper had shown up for the meeting Saina hadn't known she'd called.

Chef looked thoughtful. "I could do a dense cake and we probably have enough here to frost one over with the real stuff." He crumbled the piece in his hand and tested how well it pressed back together. "I'll have to make a binder. Sugar, probably. That will match the sparkle and set up nicely."

"Will he smell the difference?" Tex asked. "I've known some drinkers who could tell the watered-down stuff from across the bar. And they were just human."

"It will be wrapped in plastic, and the suitcase is so saturated with the stuff, I imagine it will mask the weakness of the rest," Saina guessed. "Bastian should be able to give us an idea of how well it will work."

"And if he does eat it?" Tex queried. "You don't offer a shot to a recovering alcoholic."

Saina had wrestled with the morality of every aspect of their plan. "I am bound not to work magic on him, or I could try to sing it out of him. Fortunately, goldshot works itself entirely out of the system within a few weeks of being clean, so all we have to do is see that he doesn't get a supply for a while."

"I'm not sure there's even a full dose here," Chef said. "It's enough to frost a brick, and maybe fool him, but I'm not convinced it would actually be a fix."

"We'll need to clean the outside of the suitcase," Jenny suggested, lifting the open lid with her pen.

Travis scraped a shard of the goldshot off the suitcase with one of his tools. "I can color match this. We can pack the suitcase with fake bricks and one real one."

"Almost real," Chef corrected.

"What if he grabs the wrong brick to inspect?" Laura asked.

There was a moment of silence, then Wrench, standing in the back with his big arms crossed, suggested, "Take the right one out and put it on top of the suitcase when you open the negotiations."

There was a chorus of approval for the idea.

Wrench gave a dry laugh. "It's like you've never been in on a drug deal before."

"This is a fascinating conversation to walk in on."

Scarlet stood in the doorway; none of them had even heard her open the door.

The staff froze in a tableau of guilt.

"I'm sure this proposed drug deal has everything to do with the fact that *only* my lifeguard is on duty right now, in the middle of a busy afternoon," she said mildly, looking straight at Saina.

Saina cleared her throat to formulate an explanation, but Chef beat her to the punch.

"We're all helping Miss Saina get her grandmother out of a bit of a pinch," he explained simply.

"And it's not really a drug," Travis added. "Most of it will be gypsum."

"And technically, she isn't even dealing for the false drug," Jenny added. "It's really just a standard contract negotiation with a red herring. It might not hold up in a real court, but it doesn't actually have to."

"And it's her *grandmother*," Laura insisted.

Breck joked, "We've got to get her voice back from the sea witch before the sun sets on the third day!"

Tex elbowed Breck.

"Well, she got her true love's kiss already and that didn't work," Breck protested.

Saina, still locking gazes with Scarlet, shut her mouth. She wasn't even sure how the others had gleaned so much of the story from her, but she was touched by their quick protection, if not the Disney references.

"I have something that may help you," Scarlet said mildly.

In her hand was a syringe.

Chapter 36

BASTIAN BACK-WINGED into the familiar courtyard carefully. It had been a week since his last visit here, and he was significantly healed from his last encounter with Keylor, but he wasn't entirely sure he was ready for this. Saina's gentle hand on his neck reminded him of his purpose and he opened his mouth and roared a dragon challenge.

The courtyard still had some of the damage from his last visit, he was rather glad to realize; if it had been entirely repaired, he would have felt less effective.

Keylor did not keep them waiting long.

I am surprised to see you alive, he said derisively. *But I should have known the ocean wouldn't finish you off as it would have a* real *dragon*.

Bastian lowered his neck to the ground and let Saina hop off, dragging her heavy pink suitcase behind her.

Ah. You are only here as the siren's lackey. Keylor snorted a trail of dark smoke in derision and ignored Bastian to look greedily at Saina.

I have something you want, Saina said, her audible voice humming lightly in counterpart. She unzipped the suitcase and put a single, plastic-wrapped gray brick on the top of it.

Don't attempt to enchant me, Keylor said, drawing his head back.

I already agreed once not to, Saina said, *and I keep my promises forever.* Whether she wanted to or not, she couldn't break the contract she'd made.

Keylor sniffed. *I thought by now that you had failed in your goal.*

I don't fail, Saina said loftily. *But I've had a better offer in the meantime. I'm here to see if you're willing to change the terms of our agreement.*

Bastian was sizing Keylor up as they treated. He was less impressive than Bastian remembered, and his eyes were more orange than red. Saina had been right about his access to the goldshot — he was running out. Which was why he was eyeing the suitcase with such lust.

I still have your Voice, Keylor sneered. *You dare to ask for more?*

Keep my Voice, Saina laughed. *I have my own song. What use would an old woman be to me?*

Keylor drew up. *What is it you wish to trade, then?*

The crown of Viracocha, Saina said smoothly.

Keylor's snort of laughter had flame, and Bastian, unable to stop himself, crouched to protect his mate.

Well-trained, brother-not, Keylor mocked. *Or well-sung, I should say.*

Saina let her hum raise into an aria, and snapped her fingers at Bastian. He settled back on his haunches as if against his own will.

Can we deal? Saina pushed. *Or are you wasting my time?*

You want me to steal from my parents' hoard. That's a bold request from a half-fish.

I'm a siren who knows what she wants, Saina said, inspecting one of her hands as if her nails were a hundred times more interesting than two gigantic dragons posturing at each other. *And I have other buyers if you aren't willing.*

Keylor gnashed teeth the size of her forearm, casting longing looks at the suitcase. The smell was deliciously tantalizing to Bastian, too, but he fought back the desire, reminding himself that it was only false.

Keylor's eyes narrowed then. *Why would you send my brother-not to challenge me for your Voice, if you did not desire it?*

I didn't direct him to do that, Saina said with the unmistakable ring of truth. *He's the fool who came up with that idea. The suitcase for the crown,* she repeated. *Is it a contract?*

Yesssssss, Keylor hissed angrily.

Then Saina stopped singing.

You would enter a contract to steal from our hoard?

The illusion that Saina had been holding dropped with her song, revealing two dragons, one a deep navy blue, the other a forest green, perched on the highest of the courtyard walls.

Keylor, recognizing the trap, tried to protest, *Father, I wouldn't.*

The blue dragon leaped down into the courtyard. *You entered a contract you didn't intend to keep?* He asked fiercely. *I don't know which is worse.*

Keylor, the smaller green dragon sitting above them said reproachfully.

Keylor writhed, and Bastian was not a big enough dragon not to feel smug about his discomfort.

Do you disinherit this dragon? Saina asked pointedly.

Both of his parents turned from Keylor and gave Saina their full attention. To her credit, she didn't so much as squirm.

Who are you? his mother asked, not gently.

I am Saina. Do you disinherit this dragon? she repeated.

Bastian's father glanced in disgust at Keylor, who was still belly down in the courtyard trying to formulate a defense. *Yes,* he said reluctantly, clearly angry and betrayed.

Father, no! Keylor protested. *It was not such an offense.*

Saina ignored him. *Then his hoard is forfeit to you and I will treat with you in his stead. I seek the release of my Voice.*

You will offer us this vile contraband in trade, and come here with lies expecting us to treat with you? his father protested with a snort of flame.

Neither, said Saina. *I have been entirely truthful. I told him I had my own song and asked what use she would be. I told him I had a better offer. He drew his own conclusions.*

You can't do this, Keylor snarled.

Then what do you offer? Bastian's father ignored Keylor.

The truth, Saina said. *I gave you the truth about your son.*

Bastian met his mother's luminous eyes briefly. Her glance slid away quickly.

Keylor, as furious at being ignored as he was at this unexpected turn of events, gathered himself and just as Bastian was going to risk interrupting the negotiation in warning, he leaped — not for the suitcase drenched in goldshot, but for Saina, claws outstretched.

Chapter 37

THIS MIGHT ACTUALLY work, Saina thought privately, hardly daring to hope. Dragons kept promises, but they were masterful at loopholes; that was why they made such terrific lawyers. She kept her chin high and was careful with her words. Dragon expression was hard to read, and she was watching Bastian's father carefully.

She didn't see Keylor's attack until silver claws were slashing at her.

Before she could so much as stagger backwards, Bastian was diving between them, driving into Keylor with a roar. *That is my mate!*

Saina fell back against a fountain as the two tumbled in a flurry of beating wings and lashing tails. Her hand came away from her chest bloodied, but it was quickly obvious that it was little more than a surface scratch.

She couldn't hear what Bastian was saying — it was private to Keylor only, and Keylor's responses were similarly narrow-banded, but the fight intensified. Over and over, Keylor attacked, and Bastian drove him back and released him, withdrawing and giving his brother a chance to surrender.

Keylor wanted no part of surrender.

Keylor sank teeth into Bastian's shoulder and held on like a pit bull while Bastian shook him, staggering and dragging him along a stone balustrade.

Why won't you stop them? Saina shrieked at their parents, who were both watching the fight with detachment, stepping back delicately whenever the battle grew too close.

Neither of those are our sons now, Bastian's father said coldly.

Saina balled her hands in fists at her sides. She wanted to run over and pound them on his uncaring blue scales, but she knew too much about dragon honor to believe that it would make any difference.

Bastian rolled over the cold stone, and Keylor finally let go of his shoulder. Saina was alarmed at the amount of blood, dark against his green scales. *I just put him back together*, she thought crossly.

The two dragons circled each other, snarling and flaming. Bastian limped slightly on his injured shoulder, but otherwise seemed faster and stronger than his brother.

Then Keylor paused, his attention caught by the forgotten pink suitcase. Saina saw that he was trembling, and knew that he must be feeling the withdrawal from the goldshot fiercely now.

Take the bait, she willed him, but she couldn't put any magic in it because she had promised not to.

Fortunately, she didn't have to. Keylor led their circling closer to the suitcase, and dashed at the last moment in, to snatch the plastic-wrapped brick from the top and swallow it in one fast gulp, smashing the suitcase aside.

Bastian darted forward, trying to take advantage of Keylor's distraction, but Keylor dodged him and leaped to the top of one of the walls. For a moment, Saina thought — hoped — that he would simply abandon the battle and flee. Bastian roared at him, but didn't follow, glancing back instead to assure himself that Saina was safe.

Keylor, his eyes already starting to swirl more red, snarled and jumped down upon him, wicked claws spread.

Bastian reared to meet him, wings beating for additional forward momentum as they clashed.

Saina bit her lip as they tore and flamed at each other, then ducked and took cover behind the fountain as the battle raged closer. Bastian just had to last a short while, but Keylor was stronger and faster now, Bastian's advantage gone now that Keylor had the goldshot coursing through his system.

Keylor's attacks grew stronger, and he pinned Bastian, striking dizzying blows at the side of his brother's head. Bastian flamed and writhed, wrenching free just as Keylor moved to bite him in the already wounded shoulder. His actions became more and more defensive as Keylor stepped up his attacks, darting away at the last moment to slash as he leaped out of the way.

Saina's nails cut crescents into her palms as she watched through the smoke-hazed courtyard. Each escape was narrower, each attack more enraged, and she had no idea how long Bastian would need to keep dodging.

She couldn't sing her magic into Keylor, but she could into Bastian, she realized.

She planted her feet and opened her mouth to sing.

Stronger than you've ever known,

A king lacking only a throne.

You will always be

Royalty to me.

Saina couldn't direct their battle, but she could remind Bastian of his strength. *Your hoard is better*, she whispered at him. *Your heart is truer.*

Bastian crashed with Keylor into another wall, and they were a snarling, tail-lashing, wing-beating ball of dragon together.

Did Bastian look stronger? Saina sang louder, desperate to help him, wincing at every blow and slash.

Then, just as Keylor turned to bite Bastian's briefly exposed neck, he shifted, and for one ridiculous moment, was dangling as a human from Bastian's scales, holding on only by wholly inadequate human teeth as his limbs flailed.

Chapter 38

BASTIAN KNEW HE'D MADE an error of exhaustion, just as he turned too late to protect his neck and saw Keylor lunge for him, teeth bared.

Then, finally, the substance they'd put in the goldshot brick that Saina had scraped together from her sodden suitcase took hold and Keylor was an ineffective human, surprised and dismayed by his unplanned shift.

As Keylor fell from the height of a dragon, Bastian twisted to catch him in one clawed foot.

The temptation to squeeze the life from his brother was as painfully keen as his desire for the goldshot that he still reeked of. Keylor had tried to hurt his mate, and had held her dearest relative hostage. He deserved death. He deserved painful death.

But Bastian uncurled his claws and put Keylor on the ground, then shifted to face him.

"What are you doing, brother-not?"

As a human, Keylor was less impressive than he was as a dragon; a pasty, thin man with an unpleasant sneer and a tremor in his voice.

"I have no taste for your death," Bastian said gently. "I know that goldshot can make you do vile things, and you have already been stripped of your hoard and your family. I know how that feels."

Keylor gnashed his teeth, hunched himself over miserably, then launched himself desperately at Bastian's face with an incoherent cry of rage. His eyes were still red with the goldshot, even in human form.

Bastian, with the human muscles and reflexes of a swimmer, easily backhanded him away into a wall, where he crumpled into unconsciousness.

Saina's voice had died to a cough; the courtyard was filled with acrid dragonsmoke.

Bastian turned to limp towards her, and glowing eyes appeared through the smoke above her curvy form.

Finish your bargaining, Bastian said to them. *Saina's Voice shall be returned to her safely and we will leave you in peace.*

He wondered at the authority in his own mindvoice. His parents had always awed and intimidated him, but now he found that they occupied no place in his thoughts. Only Saina mattered, and he wanted nothing but to turn his back for the final time on the place that had taught him only his weaknesses.

What did you do to Keylor? his mother asked. Was there concern in her voice? Did she love her children, or were they only parts of her own glory, little more than an extension of their hoard, to be judged for their value and nobility?

He wanted a drug, we happened to have one that would constrain him to his human form for a time. Bastian had no desire to explain that the drug had been liberated from the zoo prison of an insane shifter collector who had been hell bent on adding Bastian himself to his collection.

Trickery, his father rumbled, and Bastian found himself bracing for the pang of guilt he should feel for disappointing his progenitor. It was oddly missing. Perhaps he was more tired than he realized.

All an aside to the deal at hand, Saina swiftly interceded. *I offered you my exposure of your son's true nature in exchange for my Voice.*

They returned their attention to her as Bastian staggered the final steps to her side and took her hand in his own.

Riches are a more standard exchange for dragons, his father told her coldly. *There is no value in your part of this exchange.*

I base my offer on your past behavior, Saina said with no kindness. *You cast out your eldest son for something as trivial as compassion. Clearly you value your family reputation above any treasure.*

You are blackmailing us, his mother exclaimed. *You are threatening to tell people about Keylor's dishonor!*

Bastian felt Saina's grim smile. *Blackmail is such an ugly word.*

He tightened his hand in hers. This was the part of the plan with the most uncertainty.

You are a remarkable woman, his father said thoughtfully, and Bastian relaxed. They were impressed by Saina, as they should be. *It is a pity you are not a royal dragon. That would simplify this situation considerably.*

There is a story that sirens were once dragons, his mother added, cocking her head at Saina as she lowered her face to inspect her more closely. *Are you royalty among your kind?*

Saina looked back at the dragons without flinching or stepping back, despite her small comparative size and their impolite crowding. *We have a similar origin story*, she conceded. *But sirens do not have royalty.*

Then she laughed dryly. *But my name does mean 'princess' in Hindi.*

Bastian's parents exchanged a significant look and a private exchange, then turned to Saina.

We would accept this as fulfilling the terms of the contract, his father said proudly.

Bastian had been trying to decide which of his shoulders hurt worst, and whether he could gracefully go sit down on the bench to recover for a moment while his parents treated with Saina, then realized where the conversation had moved.

He blinked up at his father. *You... you'd take me back?*

Even as he tried to wrap his tired mind around the idea, Saina spoke.

You can't have him.

She was drawn up to her full height, tiny against his monstrous parents, and she brought them to silence with her statement.

Bastian is mine, by bonds more powerful than family blood or title, Saina snarled. *He is better than any of you, by any standards of human or dragon or siren, and you may not have him. He has a family of his own making, in a place that accepts him as he is, where he has a hoard that puts your gaudy pretension to shame, and if you try to take him from me and from his true family, I will hunt you to the ends of the earth and sing the sky down on you.*

Her words echoed in their minds and in their ears. Bastian was not sure when she had started singing the words out loud, but the magic in the courtyard was tangible and full of anger.

She took two firm steps forward. *I came here to treat for my Voice, taken from me by your dishonorable son, and you try to take from me the treasure that you discarded in foolishness. I will give you one chance and only one to redeem yourselves.*

Bastian's parents gaped at her.

Give. Me. My. Voice.

Chapter 39

"Are you sure about this?"

Bastian's parents had flown away with Keylor's limp form once the deal had been struck. Saina had even managed to make them promise to see him through his withdrawal, using every non-magic negotiating tool that she had.

Saina and Bastian stood alone in the courtyard at last.

"I'm sure," Bastian said firmly, leading her up the steps to the grand entrance.

"I don't want you to feel tricked," Saina insisted. "It isn't fair, and you shouldn't have to."

Bastian drew up at the top of the stairs. "The only thing that isn't fair about it is that they beat me to the punch and robbed me of the chance at a deeply romantic speech that I'd undoubtedly have forgotten in the panic of the moment anyway. You were saved the awkwardness of having to accept a ring from someone who looked like a beached fish with stagefright. As grievances with my parents go, this is fairly far down on the list."

Saina twisted the pearl ring on her finger and smiled foolishly. This was not the bargain she had expected to drive, but she was delighted with the outcome. The rings the dragons had produced from their hoard were surprisingly compatible with their tastes; Bastian's was a simple gold band and hers was a pearl cradled by four diamonds. It was likely that his parents felt like they were ridding their hoard of items too pedestrian to keep.

"Let's go find your Voice," Bastian told her, when all she could do was smile at him.

He took her hand, and they walked into through the modest man-sized door within the larger door.

Keylor's lair was dragon-sized at the front, but more human-sized to the rear, and a quick search revealed a set of cozy rooms. Saina's heart caught in her throat as an elegant silver-haired figure in a plush chair turned to look at them.

"My Voice!" Saina cried, and rushed forward.

"Heavens, child, it certainly took you long enough to come get me," her grandmother chided her as she rose gracefully from the chair. "And wearing that? Gracious, I hope no one sees us leaving together. I do assume you have come to free me?" The teasing, skeptical tone of her voice was achingly familiar.

Saina flung her arms around the slim figure, catching her in an impulsive embrace.

"Yes, yes," her grandmother said, patting her with exaggerated awkwardness. "I'm sure you're happy to see me."

"We *are* here to free you," Saina said, withdrawing to arm's length. "Your contract with Keylor is dissolved." She had to ask, "Was it terrible here?"

Her Voice sniffed. "The food was dreadful, and the service so spotty. Who only has maid service once a week? The internet connection was barely tolerable for streaming television, and you know how drafty and dry a dragon's lair generally is."

"We'll get you back to the ocean, my Voice," Saina told her, trying not to laugh at the glimpse of amusement in her grandmother's twinkling eyes. "But I want you to meet Bastian first. This is my grandmother, my Voice, Gita."

Bastian came forward from where he'd been lurking in their door for the reunion. He gave Gita his most winning smile and offered a hand. "Ma'am."

Gita looked him over carefully, and did not take the offered hand. "You may address me as your Voice," she conceded. The ring on his finger did not go unnoticed. "I suppose you think you are marrying my granddaughter."

Bastian's smile froze on his face. "Yes, your, er, Voiceness," he stammered. "It was part of the agreement for your release."

"Oh Saina, how dreadful for you!" Gita patted Saina's hand in pity. "I had the perfect man chosen for you. You could have drowned him afterwards, for all I cared, but he would have made beautiful little baby girls."

"My Voice," Saina said gently, covering her delicate hand with her own. "Bastian is my mate. I *want* to marry him." She wasn't sure how much of what her grandmother was saying was in jest, but she answered gravely, serious to the bottom of her soul, and thought she saw a flash of pain in Gita's face.

"Sirens don't have mates, my darling! And sirens certainly don't *marry*." Gita gave Bastian a sweeping look. "And if you did, Saina, sweetheart, I'm sure you could do better."

Poor Bastian looked like a beached dolphin, opening and closing his mouth as he struggled to find something to say.

Saina realized she was humming out of habit when Gita turned to her sharply. "Are you trying to enchant *me*, girl? You *have* learned a lot of bad habits while I was away."

"You!" Gita said imperiously to Bastian, leaning her magic into the musical word. "You may fetch the bags I have packed up in the other room."

Bastian looked befuddled, exchanged a look with Saina, and then politely nodded and walked to get her bags.

Gita watched him go. "Well, isn't that curious. A bit more to him than meets the eye."

"I told you, my Voice, he's my mate. You can't influence him."

"That sounds like a challenge," Gita murmured. "But no matter! Tell me what happened with our pod when I left. Why didn't one of the others come get me, if you were going to take so long about it?"

"Our pod dissolved when you left," Saina said sadly. "They fell into bickering and infighting, and I was the only one who cared to come free you."

"Ungrateful, the lot of them," her Voice sniffed. She patted Saina's hand again, more slowly this time, and Saina thought she saw a glimpse of sorrow in her sea green eyes before she straightened her shoulders. "I suppose you want me to come live with you, in whatever beach hovel that lifeguard will put you in?"

"You'd be welcome at Shifting Sands, my Voice," Saina said, though as she spoke, she wondered exactly how welcome she would actually be. She tried to imagine Gita working for Scarlet and it was nearly as impossible to picture as Scarlet being happy with Gita's presence.

"Oh, that's a shifters-only island resort, isn't it?" Gita said dismissively. "I've heard it's alright, if you don't have real standards."

"The food is very good," Saina said neutrally. She didn't precisely want to encourage the idea.

Gita waved an imperious hand of dismissal. "You two just take me to the ocean and *abandon* me there. I'll find a cruise ship that will take me. I need a little rest and pampering after my long imprisonment."

Saina looked around the well-appointed room, but held her tongue.

Bastian returned, laden with matching suitcases.

"Well, you are a strong one," Gita conceded. "Did you fetch the case from the bathroom?"

"Yes, Ma'am," Bastian said, holding it aloft.

"Maybe you'll do for Saina," she said with faint approval. "As long as she has heavy bags to lift."

They walked together to the courtyard. The smoke had mostly cleared, and the evening sun through the jungle sparkled on green leaves. Somewhere overhead, a toucan cried.

"Where's the car?" Gita asked, once they had reached the bottom of the entrance stairs.

"Ah, we didn't bring a car," Saina said. "I rode here on Bastian."

"I don't need dirty details like that, girl," Gita scolded.

"Bastian is a dragon, my Voice," Saina explained cautiously. "He can fly us wherever we'd like."

"A dragon?!" Gita took an unsteady step backwards, looking at Bastian with new cautiousness. Saina took her arm when she might have stumbled back on the last step.

"A dragon," Saina said firmly. "My dragon."

Gita sniffed. "This day is turning out to be more and more disappointing."

Chapter 40

"Are you sure we can just leave her here?" Bastian asked, trying not to sound as hopeful as he felt. He'd heard of nightmare in-laws, and even suspected he came with some, but nothing had prepared him for the casual, condescending cruelty of Saina's grandmother.

"My Voice will have no trouble finding whatever she needs here," Saina assured him. While they watched, a pair of deckhands leapt to their feet to gather Gita's luggage, practically tripping each other to follow close at her heels. Further down the dock, a man who'd been stacking crates abandoned his task to sweep the deck in advance of her approach.

Bastian could hear the faint strains of her song as she walked away — for good, he could not help but hope.

"Oh gosh," he said insincerely. "I don't know how we'll get in touch to invite her to the wedding."

Saina looked at him sideways. "There's going to be a wedding?"

"We did promise to get married," Bastian reminded her.

Saina blinked, heavy eyelashes over sea green eyes. "I guess I figured we'd just do a walk-in wedding somewhere. They have those in Costa Rica, don't they?"

"We could go through a wedding lawyer," Bastian said, feeling oddly disappointed. "Fill out some paperwork, show your passport and birth certificate. He rounds up some witnesses and it's done. Er, do you have a passport or birth certificate?"

Saina shrugged. "I can wave a piece of paper in front of him and convince him it's one."

"You don't... want a real wedding?" Even Bastian could hear how wistful he sounded.

She smiled at him, her true, crooked smile full of warmth and amusement. "Do *you* want a real wedding?"

Bastian scuffed a foot in the sand. "I do. I want to watch you walk down an aisle towards me. I want all our friends there to witness our vows. I want a giant reception with every fancy dish that Chef knows how to make."

Saina narrowed her eyes. "You want to outshine Tex and Travis' double wedding."

"I guess there's a little dragon competitiveness in me," Bastian admitted. "They're planning to marry early next summer after their court stuff is settled, and I was sort of thinking about an early spring ceremony."

"We'd have to invite your parents," Saina reminded him.

Bastian froze, imagining his parents at Shifting Sands. It was almost as horrifying as the idea of her grandmother. "I've changed my mind," he said swiftly. "It was a terrible idea. Wedding lawyer it is."

"I don't know," Saina teased. "Now I really like the idea. I could throw a bouquet and we could have a fancy dance. Everyone would know I was yours, and boggle at our elegance and beauty."

"Hrm," Bastian said, unconvinced.

Saina moved closer into his arms, sliding her curves along him. "You could peel me out of a fluffy white cupcake dress afterwards."

Bastian swallowed, his imagination doing plenty to fill in the picture. "I'm not sure..." he said.

"Maybe your parents wouldn't come?" Saina suggested, slipping her arms up around his neck.

Bastian kissed her, hands at her waist. "Is that a chance we're willing to take?"

"I'll risk it," Saina purred in his ear.

When he put her down at last, drawing away with bruised lips, Bastian remembered something she'd said. "My parents said that they had a story that sirens used to be dragons, and you said that you had heard a similar origin story."

Saina laughed. "It has significant differences. We say that dragons came from sirens. They were sirens — siren men — who preferred war to love. They could not reconcile their natures, and changed to shifters with two forms, one of scales and violence and one of humankind. I don't have a mermaid voice within me, not like you have a dragon. I am a siren, it's just who I am. Sometimes I have legs and sometimes, I don't."

She tapped the middle of his forehead. "It must be crowded in there."

"That's not where my dragon is," Bastian corrected, catching her hand. He pressed it against his chest, feeling the flutter of his heartbeat against her palm. "He is here, deeper, and it still felt empty before you came."

She looked at him with glowing eyes.

"Marry me," Bastian said, falling to one knee.

"We're already engaged," Saina reminded him, showing him her ring.

Bastian slipped it off her finger. "Pretend we're not," he suggested.

Saina left her hand extended. "Bastian, my love, I will marry you. I pledge my life to you."

Bastian eased the ring back onto her finger. "I love you, Saina," he said, standing up and sweeping her into his arms.

When he'd kissed her breathless, he set her back onto her feet. "Let's go home."

Epilogue

SOMEONE TO LOVE,

Someone to hold.

A prize of silver,

A treasure of gold...

Saina let the words and the magic with them fade away in the low-lit bar. She gestured for the audience to join her in the final refrain, and they did so eagerly, needing only the tiniest thread of encouragement from her magic. She convinced them that they each sounded amazing.

Someone to love,

Someone to hold.

A prize of silver,

A treasure of gold!

Saina stepped off the little stage to a round of gleeful applause and a chorus of requests.

"Fight Song!" someone yelled.

"Take Me Down!" someone countered.

"Part of Your World!" Breck hollered down from the restaurant deck above.

There was scattered laughter from the audience members who got the joke. Sania flipped the bird in Breck's direction and gave the rest of the audience a more decorous wave.

They returned to their chatter and drinks cheerfully.

"We might have to get Wrench to provide nightly concert security," Tex joked. "They adore you."

Bastian met her at the bar with a kiss. "They'd let you sing until tomorrow morning," he observed.

"I'm on the schedule for tomorrow at dawn to do a morning meditation," Saina said. "Lydia's doing some kind of certification or training until next week, and Scarlet thought I could probably fill the gap with a morning song-and-stretch sort of thing. If I don't cut them off now, I won't get any sleep first."

"Sleep is overrated," Laura said, from the far side of the bar where she was helping Tex fill drink orders. "And just try to convince me that you'll be getting any tonight. You're just looking for an excuse to head back to your room."

Saina grinned at her, aware of Bastian's arm, which was still around her waist possessively. She was wearing the evening dress that had been salvaged from her sodden suitcase, washed thoroughly clean of the last traces of goldshot.

"I am so glad you're taking over the dawn class," Jenny said, putting a tray of empty glasses down on the bar. "I am incapable of doing yoga at that hour. We spent ten minutes in the child pose this morning before I could even think of anything else to do."

Saina fabricated a yawn. "I may not do much better," she joked. "My only hope is that I won't accidentally sing a lullaby and put us all back to sleep."

She took Bastian's hand and left the cheerfully lit bar behind them as they crossed the bar deck to the staff gate.

The white gravel path past the staff gate was a ribbon ahead of them as they walked, hand-in-hand. The staff house ahead of them, aglow from within, was the home that Saina had never had, that she'd never known she wanted. She could feel the safety and harmony of Bastian's hoard from the doorstep.

The sign on the door had a dozen names crossed out, and Saina read them curiously, then left a puzzled Bastian at the edge of the kitchen to get a pen from the cup on the fridge.

She returned to the front door and in the final space at the bottom of the page, wrote, "The Den."

Bastian, watching over her shoulder, laughed. "It's perfect."

Saina returned the pen to the cup. "It is," she agreed contentedly, and she meant all of it. The name, the house, the resort, the island with its mysterious pool of magic, and most of all, the man beside her.

She turned to take his hand, and could not resist standing up on her tiptoes to kiss him. "Let's go to bed," she said.

"Bed sounds great," Bastian agreed.

Neither of them mentioned sleep, and by the time Bastian had unlocked the door to his hoard, most of their clothing had been already peeled off of each other.

Saina led him by the half unbuttoned shorts to the bed and pulled him into it over her. "My dragon," she breathed. "My mate."

Bastian managed some sort of acrobatics to remove his shorts without losing any skin contact, and was strong and firm along her as he pushed her hair back and kissed her neck. "My fish," he teased in her ear.

"Reptile," Saina countered, drawing gentle nails along his erect member.

Bastian flickered his tongue out at her, and she laughed until he kissed her again, drawing her close.

When he entered her, she knew she'd been wrong. *This* was home, not knowing where he ended and she began. *This* was home, being held in his strong arms. *This* was home, his kisses hot on her neck and his breath ragged in her ear as she arched against him. *This* was home with her mate.

A note from Zoe Chant

Thank you so much for buying my book! I hope you enjoyed Bastian and Saina's tale, and would love to know what you thought – you can leave a review (I read every one, and they help other readers find me, too!) or email me at **zoechantebooks@gmail.com**.

If you'd like to be emailed when I release my next book, please visit my webpage, zoechant.com, and sign up for my mailing list! You can also find me on Facebook and join my private group, where I share sneak previews and chat with readers. Keep reading to enjoy a special sneak preview of *Tropical Panther's Penance*, book 6 of *Shifting Sands Resort*.

The cover of *Tropical Dragon Diver* was designed by Ellen Million. Visit her webpage at ellenmillion.com for coloring pages of my characters and signed bookplates!

More Paranormal Romance by Zoe Chant

DANCING BEARFOOT. (Green Valley Shifters # 1). A single dad from the city + his daughter's curvy teacher + a surprise snow storm = a steamy story that will melt your heart.

Bodyguard Bear. (Protection, Inc. # 1). A curvy witness to a murder + the sexy bear shifter bodyguard sworn to protect her with his life + firefights and fiery passion = one hot thrill ride!

Bearista. (Bodyguard Shifters # 1). A tough bear shifter bodyguard undercover in a coffee shop + a curvy barista with an adorable 5-year-old + a deadly shifter assassin = a scorching thrill ride of a romance!

The Christmas Dragon's Mate. (Christmas Valley Shifters #1). A lonely bookkeeper in search of Christmas + a mysterious dragon shifter with a past full of pain + a beautiful snow castle hiding a ruthless enemy = one glittering Christmas romance!

Mated to the Storm Dragon. (Elemental Mates #1). A curvy artist down on her luck + a dragon shifter running out of time + a powerful enemy with an ancient grudge = a romance as hot as dragon fire!

Royal Guard Lion. (Shifter Kingdom #1). A curvy American shocked to learn that she's a lost princess + a warrior lion shifter sworn to protect her + a hidden shifter kingdom in desperate need of a leader = a sizzling romance fit for a queen!

Zoe on Audio

DANCING BEARFOOT – Audiobook - A single dad from the city + his daughter's BBW teacher + a surprise snow storm = a steamy story that will melt your heart.

Kodiak Moment – Audiobook - A workaholic wildlife photographer + a loner bear shifter + Alaskan wilderness = one warming and sensual story.

Hero Bear - Audiobook - A wounded Marine who lost his bear + a BBW physical therapist with a secret + a small town full of gossips = a hot and healing romance!

Zoe Chant, writing under other names

RAILS; A NOVEL OF TORN World by Elva Birch. License Master Bai knows better than to dream about his Head of Files, Ressa. A gritty and glamorous steampunk-flavored novel of murder, sex, unrequited love, drugs, prostitution, blackmail, and betrayal.

***Laura's Wolf* (Werewolf Marines # 1)**, by Lia Silver. Werewolf Marine Roy Farrell, scarred in body and mind, thinks he has no future. Curvy con artist Laura Kaplan, running from danger and her own guilt, is desperate to escape her past. Together, they have all that they need to heal. A full-length novel.

Mated to the Meerkat, by Lia Silver. Jasmine Jones, a curvy tabloid reporter, meets her match in notorious paparazzi and secret meerkat Chance Marcotte. A romantic comedy novelette.

Handcuffed to the Bear (Shifter Agents # 1), by Lauren Esker. A bear-shifter ex-mercenary and a curvy lynx shifter searching for her best friend's killer are handcuffed together and hunted in the wilderness. Can they learn to rely on each other before their pasts, and their pursuers, catch up with them? A full-length novel.

Keeping Her Pride (Ladies of the Pack # 1), by Lauren Esker. Down-and-out lioness shifter Debi Fallon never meant to fall in love with a human. Sexy architect and single dad Fletcher Briggs has his hands full with his adorable 4-year-old... who turns into a tiny, deadly snake. Can two ambitious people overcome their pride and prejudice enough to realize the only thing missing from their lives is each other?

Wolf in Sheep's Clothing, by Lauren Esker. Curvy farm girl Julie Capshaw was warned away from the wolf shifters next door, but Damon Wolfe is the motorcycle-riding, smoking hot alpha of her dreams. Can the big bad wolf and his sheep shifter find their own happy ending? A full-length novel.

Sneak Preview: Tropical Panther's Penance

by Zoe Chant

"WRENCH," TRAVIS SAID.

Panther shifter Warren "Wrench" Martin looked at him blankly for just a moment before he realized that the lynx shifter handyman was asking for the tool, not initiating a conversation. He dug into the toolbox between them and handed Travis the requested tool with a grunt.

He watched as Travis opened the problematic trap, and dumped the sludge out of it into a waiting 5 gallon bucket. "Ahah!" he said triumphantly, fishing a scrap of cloth out of the drain above. "I don't know what possesses people to put these things down drains, but I've found some odd stuff down here."

Travis reattached the trap. "Did you see how that worked? The most important thing is not to yank on it too hard. With a wrench and shifter strength, you can deform the pipe before you unscrew it if you aren't careful."

Wrench grunted an affirmative as Travis emerged from beneath the sink, wiping his hands.

"Let's give it a test drive," he said, and Wrench flipped the tap open.

Water poured cleanly down the drain without so much as a gurgle of protest or a drip.

Wrench wondered if the job always felt so rewarding; he had worked a long time in the shadowy persuasion business, and as well as it paid, it had never felt as victorious as any single repair he'd done with Travis.

"That did it!" Travis said with clear satisfaction.

As messy as it could be, this was clean work, and Wrench felt more fulfilled than he had in a lifetime of building a reputation for retribution and destruction.

"That's our last job for the day," Travis said putting the last of the tools back in their place. "You've got a few hours of daylight left if you want to hit the beach for a swim or something."

Wrench raised a skeptical eyebrow at him. "I ain't a swimmer," he said, picking up the toolbox before Travis could. He had done little enough of this job as it was. "But I was thinking..."

He paused, hesitant to continue, and Travis closed up the under sink cabinet and then looked at him curiously. "Spit it out, man!"

"There's a lot of broken roof tiles from the storm we're just going to piss away."

"Not much you can do with them," Travis shrugged. "You can't really repair them."

"You could... break em more." That wasn't too bad, Wrench thought. He was good at breaking things.

"And then?" Travis prompted as they closed up the cottage behind them and started hiking up to the mechanical room where Travis kept his tools.

"They'd make a nice... art piece. Like those things with tiny tiles that make a picture."

Travis blinked. "A mosaic?"

"Sure," Wrench shrugged. "It's just an idea."

"Well, yeah," Travis agreed thoughtfully. "You could just press it into wet thinset over stucco if the pieces were small enough. You got a picture in mind?"

"I dunno," Wrench growled, embarrassed. "Like a flower or a butterfly or something. They're kinda orange."

Travis did an admirable but insufficient job of hiding his amusement. "Yeah, we could do that," he agreed.

"It's something I could do," Wrench said off-handedly. "Wouldn't take more of your time."

"You ever done anything like that before?" Travis asked candidly.

"Nah," Wrench admitted, scowling. He was regretting voicing the idea.

"Let's do a little piece of the courtyard behind the spa, see how it goes, before we do it anywhere lots of people will see it. Pretty much only Lydia uses that space."

Wrench grunted, happier with Travis' agreement than he wanted to admit. "I could do that now," he suggested. "I ain't got anything else going on."

Travis's thoughts were clearly off somewhere else. Wrench looked up along the resort above them and saw one of the twins waving from the deck above. That would be Travis's mate Jenny, by his distracted grin and return wave. "Sure," Travis said.

"Knock yourself out. The ratio of water for the thinset is on the bag. Use one of the gray buckets."

"Got it, boss," Wrench said automatically.

"Not your boss, Wrench," Travis reminded him as Jenny disappeared above them. "I'm just showing you the ropes."

"Well, I'm real grateful for your helping me get this work," Wrench said gruffly. "Especially after that, er, professional misunderstanding."

He had been hired to bring Jenny's twin sister Laura back to the cartel in Los Angeles, but had mistakenly taken Jenny instead. He still wasn't entirely sure how he'd been convinced to turn on his employers for a plea bargain, but he felt like for the first time in a long time, his life had some sort of real potential.

The biggest problem he had working here at this tropical resort was the island time they seemed to be on, with long periods of leisure that didn't fit with his need to be constantly busy. He didn't want the time to think about the pending court date, and he had no interest in the luxury beach entertainment the resort offered.

Travis punched him in the shoulder and Wrench had to hold himself back from turning and pounding him into the ground in return. "You've been a great help," the lynx shifter said merrily. "And you say probably twice as much as Graham does."

Wrench grunted.

"There's that chatty nature," Travis teased.

Jenny skipped down the stairs towards them. "Scarlet is thinking about having an impromptu beach bonfire tonight, if you think the storm downed wood has dried out in the sun long enough."

"Will you dance around it nude?" Travis asked with a grin.

"Keep dreaming," Jenny told him, but she was smirking in return.

Knowing that they were aware only of each other now, Wrench left them without further comment.

LYDIA MORENO LOOKED out the small window, down at the crinkly ocean and the island growing below. She was more excited about returning to Shifting Sands Resort than she had ever been before.

"Isn't it lovely?" the little white-haired woman sitting next to her chirped, leaning over to look out the same window. "Have you ever seen such a gorgeous little island?"

"It's more beautiful every time," Lydia said with a gentle smile, sitting back so the woman could get the best view.

"Oh, you've been before?" the woman said with an appraising glance.

Lydia knew her simple clothing didn't make her seem like someone with the kind of cash to travel multiple times to a luxurious tropical resort. "I work there," she said without shame.

"What a gorgeous place to work!" the woman said with an overly friendly pat to Lydia's knee. "My goodness, you must love it! Tell me what you do!"

Lydia smiled. "I run the spa," she said proudly. "I also teach salsa and do many of the meditation and yoga classes."

"I simply must take your classes," the woman said too eagerly. "What do you like most about your work?"

"I enjoy meeting all the new people who come here," Lydia said simply. "My work is very varied, and although it is sometimes busy, I never get bored."

"Do you like the people you work with?" The woman was over-the-top nosy. "Do you get new people in very often?"

"Turnover is high," Lydia said agreeably. "Not everyone can handle the isolation. But we have a really excellent core staff that is like family."

She was glad when the woman finally turned to converse with the woman across the aisle from her, and she could politely return to watching the island grow below her.

Every time she returned from visiting with her family or renewing her certification, she felt more and more like she was coming home.

But this time was different.

This time, her mate was there.

She had always known where he was, like a faint compass pull; most swan shifters had a mate sense. The tug had always been weak enough that she'd never felt compelled to drop her life in progress to find him. Even as she got older and her younger sisters and brothers went seeking their own partners as their mate sense matured, she had waited in the wings, trying to be patient and trust that things were happening as they should.

Now, her patience would finally be rewarded, and she could not help squirming with nervous excitement.

What would he be like? A guest at a shifters-only resort, so he was a shifter, and probably well-to-do if he could afford Shifting Sands' exclusive pricing. Would he be young? Old? Blonde? Tall? Short? Would he sweep her away in a romantic dance at the next formal? Or go swimming with her at the beach at midnight?

Lydia put a finger to the cross at the base of her throat. She had to believe she would love him no matter what. She just had to trust that this was her path to happiness and have faith that they were going to be perfect for each other.

The hot tropical air that greeted her when the plane doors opened smelled amazing and charged with energy. She let the guests disembark first, struggling with their overstuffed carry-ons and exclaiming over the humid, scented air.

By the time she was off the plane, the resort van had already departed with the first batch of guests, leaving her with the second group and the extra luggage.

The white-haired woman had secured a seat on the first van trip, and the few remaining guests were sitting in the little open shelter that was the only structure at the landing strip. They seemed to be an equal mix of patiently enjoying the tropical view and feeling slighted that they were having to wait. A middle-aged brunette woman immersed a book sat between a bored-looking blonde wearing impractical heels and a young Swede. The Swede was trying to explain over her head to the blonde that he was a professional hockey player. She didn't look impressed.

A grim-faced man completed the group, and he scowled at everyone and then walked to the far end of the structure to light a cigarette. He didn't look like the sort to book a solo vacation at Shifting Sands, but they did get all kinds.

When Travis, the resort handyman, returned with the van, she enfolded him in a warm, brief hug, and then helped load the luggage in the back.

"We've got stories," the lynx shifter told her, a merry twinkle in his eyes. "So many stories!"

"I can't wait to hear them," Lydia said eagerly. He looked different, somehow, though he'd been so overworked and stressed out when she left that perhaps it was only that he'd finally gotten a decent night of sleep.

The road back to the resort was noticeably worse than it had been when she left, thanks to the storm that had just swept through, and the jaw-chattering trip was too rough for conversation, or much of anything except clinging to the side rails in the van trying not to end up on anyone else's lap.

Graham, the lion shifter in charge of landscaping, met them at the resort entrance to help unload the luggage and Lydia caught him for a quick hug as well. He gave her a dutiful kiss on the cheek and said gruffly, "Welcome back." Then he picked up more of the giant suitcases than looked possible and vanished down into the greenery.

The resort owner, Scarlet, was checking guests in and paused in her task to flash Lydia a quick welcome smile. "Meeting at three!" she called, and Lydia waved and carried her own small bag to the top of the path down into the resort.

She paused for only a moment, to soak in the familiar view. Her mate was down there, somewhere tantalizingly close, and she longed to drop her bag and fly to find him.

But she'd waited this long to meet him and she could wait a little longer. She knew that her spa would soon be busy with all the new arrivals and duty called first.

Finish the story in *Tropical Panther's Penance!*

72135305R00099

Made in the
USA
Middletown, DE